Ainsley,

Back your adventure!

[signature]

Early

Winter's

Orb

Ainsley,

Real heroes read!

[signature]

Dedication

David:
Sara, Josh, and Connor

Charlie:
Mom and Dad

Special thanks from the co-authors to Emily Asher. You've
gone above and beyond the call of duty.

ISBN 0-9728461-2-3

Printed in the U.S.A.

Second Printing, April 2005

Early Winter's Orb
Table of Contents

Fantasy Name Guide for Early Winter's Orb

In fantasy books like Knightscares, some character names will be familiar to you. Some will not. To help you pronounce the tough ones, here's a handy guide to the unusual names found in *Early Winter's Orb*.

Agamemnon
Agg - uh - mem - non

Coraleen
Core - uh - leen

Jasiah
Jay - sigh - uh

Rief
Reef (rhymes with *leaf*)

Shivasuin
Shiv - uh - soon

Sunderwraught Mountains
Sun - dur - raught (rhymes with *brought*)

Typhon
Tie - fin

Willowhill and Surroundings

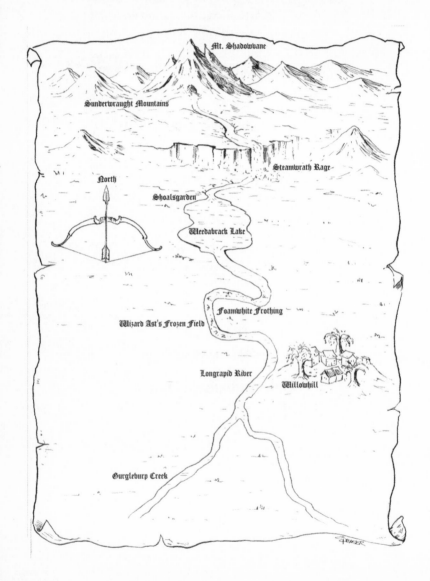

Knightscares #3:
Early Winter's Orb

David Anthony
and
Charles David

Strange Weather

1

Ffft-thew!

I love that sound. It's the noise an arrow makes when it leaves my bow on a good shot. Not too loud or too soft, and very little *twang*. When I hear it, I know my aim is perfect.

This morning I hadn't heard that sound much. The cold and snowy weather had my concentration off. There wasn't supposed to be snow for at least another month.

My parents tried to pretend that nothing was wrong or even unusual, but it was supposed to rain at this time of year, not snow.

I might be only twelve, but I knew that much. Fall had just begun. Something was terribly wrong with the weather.

I noticed the worried looks in my parents' eyes when they

glanced at the sky. Something *dangerous* was happening.

"*Woof!*" Leland barked at my side, interrupting my thoughts. He was waiting for me to tell him to fetch my last arrow.

Leland had been my best friend since my parents brought him home when I was seven. He was five now. That was thirty-five in dog years, but he still acted like a puppy.

Leland was a very big dog with lots of bushy yellow, tan, and brown fur. We weren't exactly sure what breed he was, but his feet were as wide as my Dad's hands put together, and he stood taller than my waist.

Leland was also the best guardian a girl could have. Most of the time he was a playful giant, but when I was in danger he became as fierce as a mother bear protecting her cubs.

"Emily!" Dad called from the other side of a thicket of bare trees. "It's time to leave."

"Coming!" I shouted. I scratched Leland's big head. "Fetch, boy. Go get it."

The dog bounded off through the dusty snow with his tongue hanging out, and I turned to rejoin my parents.

We'd camped the night before on our way to Willowhill, the nearest town on the Longrapid River. Normally the trip takes less than a day, but the unusual weather had slowed us down.

Except for the weather, I was excited about the trip.

Once a year, Willowhill observed the Celebration of Leaves, an autumn festival, and I was going to participate in the festival's Sling and Archery competition.

This was the first year I'd be old enough to compete, and I planned on winning. I'm not trying to brag, but no one my age was better with a bow.

Pushing my way through the snow-covered trees, I found my parents packed and ready to go. They were sitting at the front of the wagon. Dad held the horses' reins in his hands.

I guess I look like both of my parents. I'm tall and slender like Mom, but my red hair and freckles definitely came from Dad.

"Good practice, Emily?" my Mom asked from behind her wool scarf. She was bundled up tightly against the cold. "It's time to go."

I was dressed warmly, too, but I wasn't wearing a dress like she was. I never wore dresses, bonnets, skirts, or anything too girly. Archers need comfortable clothes that don't get tangled up in their legs and feet.

I usually wore boy's clothes and kept my hair in a pony-tail. Maybe that made me weird, but I liked it that way just fine. No one could shoot like me. That was what mattered.

We spent the rest of the morning slowly creaking and bumping our way to town. I passed the time by waxing my bow and straightening the feathers on my arrows.

Our wagon pulled into town late that afternoon, but the dark grey sky hid the sun. A light snow continued to fall.

As its name suggests, Willowhill was built on a tall, round hill surrounded by willow trees. Some of its buildings even have great tree trunks growing in and around their walls.

"Here, take this to pay Mr. Barleyhop for our room," Dad told me. "Your mother and I will stable the horses." A small leather coin purse dangled from a thin cord in his hand.

I snatched the purse eagerly and attached it to my belt. "You got it!" I said. "I'll meet you there. C'mon, Leland."

Mr. Barleyhop owned the Eternal Flame Inn, the biggest and best inn in town. People from miles around stayed there during the Celebration of Leaves.

Best of all, my friend Daniel would be there. He was an orphan, but Mr. Barleyhop allowed him to live at the inn in exchange for doing odd jobs.

The inn was so crowded that I could barely push my way into the common room. That was where guests gathered to eat, drink, talk, tell stories, and listen to music.

People stood around discussing the strange weather in quiet voices. None of them seemed happy. It didn't feel the way it usually did right before the Celebration of Leaves.

When I spotted Mr. Barleyhop across the room, I sent

Leland ahead to cut a path through the crowd.

I reached for my coin purse and found it—

Gone!

Someone had stolen my gold!

Human Shadow

2

What was I going to do? Someone had stolen my coin purse and gold. Without them, I couldn't pay Mr. Barleyhop for a room. Our trip to Willowhill was ruined!

The common room suddenly felt smaller, and I realized that I was surrounded by strangers. There was a thief nearby. It could be anyone.

Men with shaggy beards and faces wrinkled from working in the sun spoke in deep voices. Women glanced at me and whispered to one another. I didn't recognize anyone, and their dark conversations made me uncomfortable.

"It's the end of the world ..." a woman shuddered.

"... unnatural snow ..." a man muttered, shaking his head.

"... Longrapid River running backward," said someone I couldn't see.

Everyone sounded worried and tense. A soft whisper right in my ear startled me.

"I'm a human shadow."

"*Who* ...?" I spun around, but there was no one there. At least no one paying any attention to me.

I wanted to scream. Hadn't anyone noticed that I'd been robbed? Hadn't anyone seen the thief leaning over my shoulder?

I tried to calm down by taking a deep breath. That was when I saw him. The thief. He hurriedly slipped through a door labeled *private* and disappeared.

I only caught a quick glance, but he wore a dark hood pulled over his head and was moving fast. He was definitely up to no good.

I didn't wait. I had to get my coin purse back. With Leland serving as my personal battering ram, I struggled through the crowd.

People muttered as I pushed my way past, but Leland's size quieted them. No one wanted to disturb the giant-of-a-dog.

The private door was unlocked, and we entered. I'd have unslung my bow from my shoulder if I'd thought it would be of use indoors.

Although I'd stayed at the Eternal Flame with my parents many times, I'd never been through the private door. I'd always wondered what might be hidden on the other side.

Finally knowing was a disappointment. The room wasn't large or full of gleaming treasures the way I'd imagined. It was a small library.

Books lined shelves on two walls, and a torch burned above a small fireplace on a third wall. For some reason, the torch didn't give off any smoke, and its flame had a greenish tint.

I sighed heavily. The room was empty except for Leland and me.

"Guess we lost—"

Vrooosh!

A section of a bookcase suddenly slid open like a door, startling me. Darkness filled the space beyond.

"I told you I was a human shadow," said a familiar voice.

3

I took a step back and peered into the darkness beyond the secret door. The light from the torch behind me didn't brighten the area at all. The doorway was black.

"Guard," I commanded Leland, but he just glanced at me curiously. He didn't seem to sense any danger.

A quiet snicker drifted out from the darkness. Then it turned into a loud chuckle. My friend Daniel stepped through the doorway, his smiling face flushed with amusement.

"Lose something, Emi?" he asked with a smug grin. He twirled my coin purse by its string around one finger.

"*Emily*," I corrected firmly, planting my hands on my hips. Daniel liked to shorten my name to *Emi*, especially when he teased me. Which was often. He was always making jokes and acting like a wise guy.

16

That's why I liked him so much.

He also liked to call himself a *human* something or other. Like *human shadow*. That was his favorite saying. I should have thought of it sooner.

"These are dangerous times, Emi," he continued, ignoring what I'd said. "Snow is falling. The Longrapid River is running backward."

He shrugged. "One must be cautious with valuables."

Fwoo-fwoo. My coin purse continued to spin around his finger, and he grinned. He was acting like a know-it-all, but I was going to turn the tables on him.

"If *one* doesn't give back my coin purse," I said all syrupy, "*one* will feel my boot against *one's* shin."

Daniel's grin widened, but I turned to Leland before he could respond.

"Pounce," I instructed.

In a blur of fur and muscle, Leland hunched back and leaped. Daniel didn't stand a chance. He crumpled beneath Leland's weight.

My coin purse landed with a *chingle*, and I scooped it up. "We thank *one*," I smirked. "Heel, Leland."

Leland licked Daniel's face sloppily then bounded to my side. I continued to smirk.

Daniel wasn't flustered. In one speedy motion, he rocked back on his shoulders, pushed his hands flat against the floor over his head, and sprang to his feet.

17

He winked at me. "Glad you finally made it to town," he said.

Besides being a smart-alec, Daniel liked to think of himself as an acrobatic jack-of-all-trades. A *rogue*, he called it. Sneaky, fast, clever, and always one step ahead of the other guy.

Sometimes he really was a human shadow. He was as good at being sneaky as I was at shooting a bow.

Daniel was my age and height. He was kind of thin and wiry like a wolf cub that hasn't grown into its body, and he had black hair with long bangs.

"The weather slowed us up," I explained, but I really didn't want to talk about the snow or the river running backward. If I didn't talk about those things, I could pretend they weren't happening.

"What is this place?" I asked to change the subject.

Daniel spread his arms and bowed to me and then to Leland. The dog yawned and laid his head down between his paws.

Sometimes I wished I knew what Leland was thinking. It would be so fun if he could talk.

"This room," Daniel announced, ignoring Leland, "is just about the most important place in Willowhill."

I rolled my eyes. Knowing Daniel, he was exaggerating or joking, or both.

"I supposed it's important because you're standing in it,"

I said without cracking a smile.

He frowned and put a hand over his heart, pretending to be hurt. "That's the second reason," he grinned. "The first is because of that." He pointed at the smokeless torch on the wall. "The Eternal Flame."

I stared at the torch. It didn't look all that remarkable to me. The torch was set in a tarnished brass holder and looked to be very old.

"Looks can be misleading," Daniel added.

I turned to him again, but he'd vanished. Then I felt a tap on my shoulder. Daniel was sneaking again.

"The Eternal Flame can never go out," he whispered mysteriously. "It burns and burns all by itself … forever."

I glanced at the torch and felt a tingle run up my spine. Daniel was talking about magic.

The Eternal Flame had never gone out, and Daniel claimed that it couldn't be extinguished.

Of course that was before I got my hands on it. I found a way to extinguish it right when we needed it most.

To Arms!

4

"To arms! To arms!" came an urgent cry from the common room.

"There's terror in the harbor!" shouted another voice.

Before I could react, Daniel threw open the door and sprinted out. Leland and I charged after him.

The inn's entrance was open, and two armored men stood panting in the doorway. Clumps of wet snow filled the grooves of their armor.

"The Longrapid River has dragged a monster up from the sea," one of the soldiers explained. "It's destroying the harbor."

"All who are able, come quick," beckoned the second.

The soldiers spun around and vanished into the snow outside. Their repeated cries of warning echoed through the streets.

My time to ignore the strange weather was over. Not only was the Longrapid River running backward, but it had pulled something terrible up from the sea far to the south.

Daniel grabbed my arm and squeezed. "We've got to help," he told me. There wasn't even a trace of joking in his voice.

I nodded numbly, and then the three of us pushed our way through the common room. Half of the people there stumbled back in terror. The other half drew weapons and scrambled for the door.

Outside, the three of us turned down a side street and Daniel led the way. He lived in Willowhill and knew its streets and alleys better than I did.

The harbor was located on the edge of town at the base of a steep hill. Looking down upon it, we froze from shock rather than cold.

"*Human* …" Daniel gasped. Leland flattened his ears against his head and growled.

In the churning waters of the harbor thrashed an enormous dark shape. A dozen rubbery tentacles flailed around its body.

GRONK-WHOMP! The sea monster bellowed deafeningly.

An inky cloud swirled about the creature, making it difficult to see clearly. But I saw enough of the horrible scene along the water's edge. Too much. I wanted to shut my eyes and drive the memory of it from my mind.

I wanted to scream. When Daniel did, I joined him.

Shaped like a bloated octopus, the beast lashed out with its tentacles again and again. They coiled around river boats, crushing them as if they were sand castles, and snapped like whiptails against targets on the beach.

The town's defenders battled from the docks and shore-line, but they were clearly outmatched. Their weapons were tiny next to the sea monster and inflicted little damage.

They didn't stand a chance. The whole harbor, and then the town, would be destroyed.

GRONK-WHOMP! The monster roared again as it slammed a boat against some rocks. Jagged streaks of lightning crackled like hissing snakes along its tentacles, igniting fires where they struck the docks and boats.

"*W*-what is that *th*-thing?" Daniel sputtered.

I shook my head in disbelief. Tentacles, lightning, a cloud of misty ink—I'd never imagined such a creature.

Summoning my courage and counting on my hours of archery practice, I unslung my bow, loaded an arrow, and took aim.

I prayed I'd hear the *ffft-thew* sound when I fired. The shot would be the most important of my life.

I swallowed slowly, ignoring everything around me but the creature. Leland, Daniel, and the town's other defend-

ers melted from my vision. I saw nothing but the terrible beast and felt nothing but my bow.

Directly ahead, a serpentine tentacle rose from the misty ink then dipped into a curve like the letter *S*. Pale, big fish eyes as glassy as a corpse's stared up at me.

In horror, I realized that the creature's tentacles weren't arms. They were necks. Each one of them ended in the head of a giant vicious eel.

The monster was more awful than I'd thought.

I wanted to scream again. I wanted to run. But somehow I held my arms steady and started to draw.

Arick Dragonsbane

5

Now! my mind shouted. *Fire!*

My fingers let go just as a strong hand with a grip like iron grasped my forearm. The contact sent my shot zipping harmlessly off into the snow.

"Stay your hand, lass!" ordered a commanding voice. "I prefer not to be shot in the back."

Startled, I turned to see the biggest man I'd ever seen. He towered over me as if he was a giant and I was standing in a hole.

"Arick Dragonsbane at your service," the man boomed. "Arrows are no match for a tidal hydra. Let me take care of this."

The big man hoisted an enormous, barbed harpoon in his right hand. It must have been as tall as a man sitting on horseback.

Arick's face and chin were covered by a braided blond beard, but I still spotted a grin beneath his whiskers.

"*S*-sure thing," I stammered, not knowing what else to say. Arick seemed friendly but his size made him almost as terrifying as the tentacled creature below.

The tidal hydra, I silently corrected myself. That's what Arick had called it.

With a wink and quick nod, he charged down the hill. His thunderous voice belted out a fierce battle cry as he ran.

Raise sword and spear.
Rear battle gear.
Hear the hero's call.

With mind and might,
Smite evil's blight.
Right the wrongs for all.

When Arick's chant ended, Daniel gasped. "Do you know who that is?"

I shrugged. "Arick Dragonsbane?" I didn't know the man any more than I knew the tidal hydra, but I wasn't about to give Daniel a reason to tease me.

"Arick—yeah," he said doubtfully, squinting at me. He suspected I'd never heard of Arick Dragonsbane. Which I hadn't.

"He's just about the most famous hero there is, Emi," Daniel explained. "He'll take care of that hydra."

GRONK-WHOMP! The tidal hydra bellowed as if in challenge to Daniel's words, and we anxiously peered over the hill's snow-covered edge with our fingers crossed.

Arick slipped and slid as he made his way down, but after each stumble he was back on his feet in an instant. I'd never expected such a big man to move so quickly.

When the town's defenders saw him coming, they cheered excitedly and pulled back to safety. Apparently they had as much faith in him as Daniel did.

From the edge of the shoreline, Arick faced the hydra alone. It loomed above him like a hungry, living mountain.

"Be gone, sea-spawn!" he roared while jabbing his harpoon forward threateningly. "You do not belong here!"

GRONK-WHOMP! The hydra replied. Then with blazing speed, it lashed out a tentacle. The head on its end was a mass of razor-like teeth and frothy drool like the foam on a beach.

Arick dropped to one knee and brought up his huge harpoon to block the attack.

Gzzzttt-clang!

Lightning flashed between the hydra and harpoon with a piercing, metallic clash. Popping and hissing sparks streaked the air like fireworks.

Grunting loudly, Arick carefully deflected the blow and rolled forward, tucking into a somersault before leaping to his feet.

"You'll have to do better than that!" he challenged.

My jaw dropped at his courage. Arick Dragonsbane had to be the bravest man alive!

Or the craziest.

Bolts of lightning popped and sizzled along the hydra's tentacle-necks, but silence fell over everything else. Even the snow stopped falling.

My chest tightened and I couldn't keep from shouting. "Now, Arick!"

Arick half-turned to look up the hill. That's the last I saw of him before the hydra attacked again.

Roaring like tidal waves, the sea monster's twelve fanged mouths opened wide and belched forth a dozen funnels of dark ink. They erupted like jets of flame from a dragon.

Urgently, Arick dove to avoid the funnels, but twelve attackers were too many. Twisting and spinning to his right, he disappeared in the mass of inky black.

All twelve of the hydra's heads reared in victory.

GRONK-WHOMP!

HARRR-RONK!

6

"*Nooo*!" I shrieked.

The heavy ink cloud filled the harbor, flashing with lightning like an angry thunderhead. I couldn't see anything in the darkness, and I felt as useless as a bow without a string.

Arick had disappeared and the cloud was spreading.

"Arick needs us," I said, grabbing Daniel's arm. He was staring down the hill with a blank look on his face.

I squeezed his arm harder. "Come on!"

Daniel blinked, then glanced at me with a determined look in his eyes. "Lean on me," he said. "I'm a human balancing act." That meant he supposedly wouldn't slip.

Together we started down the hill, clutching one another's sleeves for balance. *Human balancing act* or not, Daniel leaned on me as much as I leaned on him.

Leland bounded ahead of us, barking in short bursts like a parent reminding us to be careful.

Halfway down the steep hill, a tremendous bellow stopped us in our tracks. We slid awkwardly to a halt.

HARRR-RONK!

It was the tidal hydra again, but it sounded different. Had the sound been a roar of triumph? Had it defeated Arick? *Killed him?*

My heart missed a beat and my chest went as cold as the snow. Arick couldn't be dead!

I wanted to run to save Arick, but I couldn't move my legs or even blink my eyes. I huddled with Daniel on the hillside, shivering and watching the inky cloud swirl and flash.

HARR ... the hydra rumbled, sounding quieter and somehow distant. The lack of intensity in the noise gave me hope.

"*Arick* ... ?" I whispered between my chattering teeth.

There was still no sign of him. My fingernails stabbed into Daniel's arm as I squeezed harder, anxious for a sign of Arick.

Then the cloud parted and Arick stepped clear, coughing heavily. He leaned wearily on his harpoon, and his beard glistened with sweat. Scorch marks and black ink covered his clothing and armor.

When he saw us, he gave a quick wave then collapsed to

his knees. Behind him, the hydra's cloud slowly scattered like the smoke from a dying fire. The harbor's waters calmed, and there was no sign of the tidal hydra.

Arick had done it! He'd single-handedly defeated the tidal hydra.

I couldn't keep from smiling. My whole body tingled with excitement. Willowhill was safe and Arick was alive.

"I told you," Daniel beamed at me. "Arick's a human army."

I nodded in eager agreement then looked down the hill again.

The smile melted from my lips.

Arick was lying face-down in the snow, not moving at all. Willowhill was safe, but what price had Arick Dragonsbane paid?

From Avalanche to Anchor

7

Big flakes of snow began falling again as I watched the prone form of Arick Dragonsbane. The hero of Willowhill still wasn't moving.

Leland sank to his stomach in the snow and whimpered as if he understood what had happened. His ears drooped sadly.

When I reached out to pat him reassuringly, I noticed that Daniel was missing and glanced up worriedly. *Where is he this time?*

"Clear the way!" he shouted from somewhere uphill as if in answer to my question.

I turned around in time to see him barreling down the slope. He was riding a long wooden toboggan, its ropes clutched in his hands like a horse's reins. Snow sprayed into the air behind him.

Sluuuuuush! He whizzed past me on the sled. His face was red from the cold and wind, but he was smiling. From over his shoulder, he shouted to me.

"I'm a human avalanche!"

He meant as fast as an avalanche, but I couldn't help thinking about the *crash* of an avalanche. Daniel would never be able to stop before splashing into the freezing water of the harbor. What was he doing?

Townsfolk crowded around Arick. They'd rolled him over, and a woman knelt next to him carefully checking for injuries.

Daniel flew past them in a flurry of white.

Here comes the crash, I thought, cringing and smirking at the same time.

"*Maaaaaah!*" Daniel cried, sounding so much like a baby screaming for its mother that I decided to tease him about it later.

Just before crashing into the water, he twisted in his seat and tried to dive backward. He might have made it, too, if his foot hadn't been tangled in the toboggan's rope.

As the toboggan shot off shore, Daniel sailed right along with it. For a brief moment the two were airborne. Daniel's arms and legs windmilled wildly and his mouth and eyes formed astonished *O* shapes.

Then he crashed into the harbor with a splash. Water and bits of ice erupted into the air.

Leland scrambled to his feet and wagged his tail. *"Ar-ar-ar-arf!"* he barked playfully. It was dog laughter. For once I knew what he was thinking.

"He's alive!" someone shouted from the shoreline. It was the woman who'd been tending Arick's wounds. She waved her hands and called to the townsfolk gathered at the top of the hill. "Arick Dragonsbane is alive!"

If Daniel hadn't been sloshing about in the harbor like a wet cat, I might have cried. I didn't know Arick well, but his battle with the tidal hydra had proved that he really was a hero.

Feeling a lump in my throat but smiling anyway, I scratched Leland's back. "Come on, boy, let's fish that *human anchor* out of the water."

Symptoms

8

A short while later, the common room of the Eternal Flame was more crowded than ever. Its occupants were grumbling louder, too.

Leland and I sat with my parents at a small table in the back of the room. Daniel sat alone on the stairway that led to the guest rooms upstairs. He huddled in a tattered wool blanket, appearing completely miserable.

He's probably still cold from the river, I thought, but the sour look on his face told me he didn't want company.

I felt bad for him. Aside from Mr. Barleyhop, he didn't have any family. When he'd jumped on the toboggan, he'd been trying to demonstrate something to himself and to the citizens of Willowhill.

He'd wanted to rescue Arick and get himself noticed.

Most people don't pay attention to orphans. They think

kids like Daniel are someone else's problem. What Daniel needed to know was that people cared about him whether he was a hero or not.

Right then, Arick was speaking to the gathering in the common room. He had a lot to say, and none of it was good.

Like Daniel, he wore a blanket draped over his shoulders. He sat on the warm stones of the hearth with his back to the fire and a steaming cup of tea in his hand.

"People of Willowhill," he rumbled in his deep voice. "This afternoon I arrived just in time—"

"Just in time to give that hydra the what-for!" shouted Gram Blathersome, an elderly woman known for talking too much. A round of cheers and applause erupted throughout the crowd.

Arick smiled briefly at the praise but had a faraway look in his eyes. When the crowd quieted, he continued.

"I arrived in time to warn you," he said, raising his voice, "of a terrible danger to the north. From Mount Shadowvane in the Sunderwraught Mountains."

"More dangerous'n that hydra?" Gram Blathersome interrupted again with a confident cackle.

This time Arick frowned at Gram, and the crowd went silent. Gram fidgeted in her seat and cleared her throat noisily. "Worse'n the snow?" she offered without much enthusiasm.

Arick met her gaze and Gram looked away quickly. "The *danger* of the snow," Arick said somberly.

Hushed whispers swept through the crowd. The townsfolk had thought the weather *odd* but not necessarily *dangerous*.

"The untimely snow," Arick continued, "and the strange current of the Longrapid River are connected. I'm afraid the tidal hydra was not our greatest problem."

The crowd gasped again, even Gram Blathersome. No one could believe that something more dangerous than a tidal hydra was coming.

Arick stood up, slipping the blanket from around his shoulders and quickly finishing his tea. "I arrived in time to warn you, but now I am late. I must depart immediately for the nearby town of Tiller's Field. Wizard Ast is expecting me."

I'd never met Wizard Ast, but I'd heard all about him. He had a funny way of repeating himself when he spoke, and had once been turned into a frog by a witch's spell.

If Arick had to visit him, things were really bad. Ast was the wisest and most powerful wizard around.

"Take heed, people of Willowhill," Arick warned, "for with the snow comes a terrible foe." He paused to make sure everyone was listening.

"Snow beasts run with the storms. They are fearsome monsters that cannot be killed, at least not that I have

37

seen." His eyes flickered over the crowd. "They are not flesh and blood, and weapons do not harm them."

People started muttering and whispering fearfully. Mothers and fathers clutched their children protectively.

Arick took three long strides toward the door then turned to face the crowd.

"You will know the beasts by their howls," he advised. "When you hear them—*run*. Lock up your homes and stay indoors."

He pulled open the door and started through it. In a loud voice, he said, "I will return as soon as I am able." Then he squeezed through the doorway and vanished into the dark, snowy night.

I stared after him for a long time. Mom and Dad were whispering. Mr. Barleyhop was trying to calm the crowd.

I didn't hear a word of what any of them said. I was too busy thinking about snow beasts. Horrible, howling snow beasts coming down from the mountains.

What were we going to do?

A Short Sleep

9

"Emily, are you listening?" my father asked for the third time. His strong hand shook my shoulder.

He'd asked the question two times before, but I had been too stunned to respond. Normally I felt pretty confident and safe. I had Leland and my bow. There wasn't much that could scare me.

Leland and I had even chased off a pair of no-good goblins a few weeks ago. They'd looked like they'd seen a ghost, even if one of them had been wearing an eyepatch.

But snow beasts were different than goblins. My arrows and Leland's barks wouldn't chase them away.

"Emily?" my mother asked worriedly.

I blinked. "*I*-I'm all right," I mumbled. "Sorry for blanking out on you. I was thinking."

"That's fine, dear," Mom said, patting my arm. "We're

all afraid."

Afraid? That was an understatement. How could I be *just* afraid when all I saw was a howling snow beast reaching for me with its icy fingers every time I closed my eyes?

"Now go upstairs, both of you, and lock the door," my father said. "Mr. Barleyhop is organizing a defense of the inn. We'll be all right." He tried to sound confident, but I could still hear the fear in his voice.

Mom almost jumped to her feet. Being behind a locked door must've sounded like a really good idea to her.

I didn't move. "Dad, I have my bow. And Leland. We can help." I was afraid of what was happening, but that wasn't going to stop me from helping to defend the town.

He shook his head. "Emily, go with your mother," he said firmly.

"But—" I protested.

"*Go*," was all he said. His tone told me not to argue anymore.

With a sigh, I stood up and patted my thigh, beckoning Leland to follow. I might've been willing to fight the snow beasts, but I wasn't going anywhere without Leland.

Mom kissed the top of dad's balding head, then we went upstairs. Daniel wasn't sitting on the stairs anymore, and I wondered where he'd gone.

Probably devising some crazy scheme, I thought as I collapsed onto my bed with another sigh. Leland hopped up and flopped down on my feet.

Knowing Daniel, he would probably come up with a plan to trick the snow beasts. He'd convince them that we were all human torches so they'd stay away.

Mom blew out the candles in our room but left one burning for a bit of light. "Goodnight, Emily. Don't be afraid to wake me if you need me." She kissed me on the forehead.

"Thanks, Mom. I won't. Goodnight."

Human torches, I kept thinking as I tossed and turned, trying to sleep. The idea wasn't so bad. Fire melted snow. Maybe Arick hadn't tried that against the snow beasts.

If I could come up with a way to turn my arrows into torches, I could save Willowhill, I wished.

When I finally fell asleep, I dreamed of a blinding white storm. Snow and hail streaked the air like the tidal hydra's lightning. In a panic, I started to run.

Insane howls bayed from every direction. They wailed hauntingly in my ears and sent cold shivers running up my spine.

I ran harder, shrieking at the top of my lungs for Leland. But he wouldn't come and I was lost. Deep snow slowed my legs, making my limbs sluggish. I could barely move, and the howls were getting closer.

Suddenly, a dingy white hand the color of dirty snow appeared out of the storm. Long bluish fingernails of solid ice clawed at my face.

I tried to scream again but couldn't. The snow beast's icy hand covered my mouth.

Eyes Surprise

10

Kicking my arms and legs furiously, I came awake with a muffled shriek. I wasn't dreaming now, but the cold hand was still over my mouth.

There was a snow beast in my room!

My eyes popped open to see—

Daniel.

He was standing above me with one hand over my mouth and the other touching a finger to his lips for silence. The hard look in his eyes told me he wasn't playing around.

I nodded slowly to let him know I understood, and he lowered his hands.

"Get dressed and meet me in the hall," he whispered mysteriously, stepping quietly toward the door. "Be sure to bring your bow." Making as little noise as a shadow, he closed the door as he left.

I sat up and blinked until I could see in the dim light. The moon glowed softly through the window. It was the middle of the night.

Why was Daniel here now? I wondered. *And how did he get past the locked door?*

Leland stirred on the foot of my bed, still asleep.

That made even less sense. Leland was my guardian. Why hadn't he awakened when Daniel had come into the room?

Daniel's words from earlier popped into my head. *I'm a human shadow*, he'd said just before sneaking off with my coin purse.

Maybe he really was. How else could he sneak past the keen ears of a watchful dog?

Still curious, I hurriedly dressed, fetched my bow and quiver, and gave the room a final look in case I'd forgotten anything. My mother's bed was empty.

Instead of worrying, I felt angry. Something strange was going on and everyone seemed to know about it except me. Daniel was sneaking around, Mom had gotten up and left, and Dad hadn't come to bed.

Whatever was happening, I was the last to know.

Typical, I fumed. *Don't tell Emily what's going on. She's just a girl.*

I stormed out of the room and rounded on Daniel in a huff. My face felt hot and must have been red as I pointed at him angrily.

"Now you listen here, Mr. Human …"

I never finished.

My words died on my lips when I spotted Gram Blathersome standing in the hallway. She wasn't moving, and the hall was freezing cold.

Gram crouched near an open window, seeming to peer at something beyond. Her frail arms were drawn up in front of her face as if she saw something horrible. Snow gathered on the floor about her feet and on the window's ledge.

Shivering, I took a cautious step toward her. "Gram?" I croaked so quietly that I couldn't be sure I'd made a sound at all.

I took another step and slowly reached out with one quivering hand. *Maybe she didn't hear me*, I tried to convince myself. *Maybe if I tap her on the shoulder she'll turn around.*

"I wouldn't do …" Daniel tried to warn me, but I wasn't listening. I had to find out what was happening.

One more step.

Trembling, sweating even in the cold, my fingers brushed Gram Blathersome on the shoulder. That soft touch brought the worst pain of my life.

Icy heat like a frozen flame seared into my fingertips, sending a stinging shock all the way up my arm. I cried out and fell back against the wall with my hand clutched to my chest. Frosty white plumes of smoke steamed from my fingertips.

What's wrong with Gram? What had touching her done to my hand?

Gram's thin body creaked like an ice-covered tree blown by a strong wind. It rocked forward once then toppled backward into the snow on the hallway floor. Her body didn't twitch once. Gram was as unmoving and lifeless as a statue.

Her stiff body remained frozen in the same position and was coated in a thin sheet of bluish ice. Her arms still covered her face, and she was slightly bent at the waist.

But her eyes ... her terrible eyes. They flickered rapidly back and forth like the eyes of a cornered animal.

Gram was frozen alive!

Nothing else in the hallway moved. I wasn't even breathing.

Brrr-roaw! An icy howl roared up from below the window.

11

"Hurry," Daniel said, grasping my elbow. "We have to go. *Now*. There's nothing we can do for her."

Feeling as frozen as Gram, I didn't move. The howl of the snow beast had sent a paralyzing chill up my spine.

A snow beast was near, and it couldn't be stopped. It would freeze us in an instant.

"Come on!" Daniel roared, tugging my arm. "I have a place where we can hide, but we have to hurry."

I nodded mutely, still too terrified to speak. Without a word, I pointed for Daniel to lead and then patted Leland's big head. The dog's presence made me feel better. I could always count on him, even with snow beasts and their frozen victims nearby.

Brrr-roaw! The snow beast howled again. The noise was closer and broke me out of my frightened stupor.

"Go!" I cried, shoving Daniel's shoulder. "Make like a *human coward* and run!"

Daniel didn't need to be told twice. He pulled a slim dagger from his belt and started sprinting down the hall toward the stairs. When the snow beast howled a third time, Leland and I were right on Daniel's heels.

Panting and sweating despite the cold, we skidded to a stop in the common room. A horrifying sight twisted my stomach into a knot worse than my dream had.

Icy townsfolk stood frozen in various positions all around the room. Men and women with weapons drawn looked like cold blue statues commemorating some historical battle. Frozen Mr. Barleyhop was there along with a few other people I recognized.

Whenever I made eye contact with one of them, their eyes shifted fearfully back and forth in a silent plea for help.

They were alive but powerless, and I forced myself to look away. I couldn't help them, and their terrified eyes frightened me.

Squinch.

I froze when a soft sound came from behind me. It sounded like a boot crunching in the snow.

A wide shadow filled the inn's open doorway. Even before seeing it, I felt it fall over me like freezing drizzle.

"Behind you!" Daniel shouted in warning.

I whipped around, sliding my bow off my shoulder and notching an arrow in one practiced motion.

A burly snow beast stood in the doorway. It was seven feet tall and all muscle. Long arms hung past its knees, ending in sharp claws, and its skin was like dirty snow mixed with blue ice.

A flash of shiny metal glinted as Daniel's dagger streaked over my shoulder toward the beast. It struck the monster square in the throat.

"Good—!" I started to cheer but ended up gasping. Daniel's dagger passed right through the snow beast with a breezy *foophf.*

There was no blood or cut. The hole closed instantly, and the unharmed beast reached for us with its thick, powerful arms.

Brrr-roaw! it bellowed eagerly.

I lowered my bow, turned, and ran.

Inside the library, Daniel slammed the door shut. The flickering green light of the Eternal Flame stung my eyes.

"The passage behind the bookshelf," Daniel panted, bracing himself against the entry door. He leaned against it with his knees bent for support. "We aren't safe here. The door locks from the outside."

My eyes widened in understanding.

The snow beast would smash through the door any second. Even if we worked together, we wouldn't be

49

enough to keep the beast out.

I dashed to the bookcase and started randomly tilting and turning books, tearing them off the shelves. "How? *How?*" I wailed. Weren't secret passages behind bookshelves supposed to open when you fiddled with the books on them?

"Fourth book on the fourth shelf!" Daniel shouted.

I obediently snatched the book, pulling it out, but nothing happened. There were no words or pictures on its cover. It was as plain as could be.

Thump!

A heavy crash shook the entry door, almost knocking Daniel to the ground. Leland barked and started to growl. Unlike the last time we'd been in this room, he sensed danger now.

"The book!" I wailed in frustration. "What am I sup- posed to do with it?"

One Arm Less

12

I stared uncomprehendingly at the ancient book in my hands. Its discolored pages were blank, like its cover. How could it help us open the secret passage behind the bookshelf?

"Daniel, *what* ... ?" I mumbled in confusion, half turning to him.

He'd thrown his hands against the doorframe for extra leverage. His face was red with strain.

"It's not a *real* book," he gasped. "Put it back on the shelf upside down—*quick*."

Clumsy with nervous excitement, I struggled to get the book in place. I heard a soft *snick* once I'd finally maneuvered it into position, and then the whole bookshelf swung slowly toward me.

The secret passage was open!

Whoooomp! The snow beast crashed into the door again, cracking it this time. One more blow would probably shatter the whole door.

"It's open!" I exclaimed.

"*Gah*—Emi!" Daniel sputtered raggedly at the same time.

As I turned, my excitement faded. The entry door was partially open and the muscled white-blue arm of a snow beast clawed through the opening. Sharp fingernails tore frantically at the wood of the door, scratching and gouging its surface.

Daniel knelt before the door with his chest, head, and arms pressed against it. His eyes were squeezed shut in concentration.

He was doing his best, but he wouldn't be able to hold out for long. The snow beast outweighed him by at least seven or eight times. His strength and determination were no match for the creature's size.

For an instant I thought of my bow but quickly remembered how Daniel's dagger hadn't even left a scratch on the snow beast. My arrows were useless.

So I improvised.

"Coming!" I yelled.

"Don't let it touch you!" Daniel cried.

I charged across the room like a mad bull, leading with my shoulder. That door was going to close one way or another.

Blammmp! I slammed into the door and heard a piercing squeal then nothing else. My world turned black and silent. Time drifted without meaning.

From somewhere deep inside, I knew that my body had collapsed onto the floor. But I felt no pain. I was in a quiet, faraway place.

Then a roaring filled my ears as if my head was underwater. Someone was talking nearby and shaking my shoulders. Something licked my cheek.

"Get up, get up!" Daniel hissed.

"*Yip*," Leland agreed, sounding as tiny as a puppy.

My eyes fluttered open, and I winced at my throbbing head. Daniel crouched over me with a strange expression on his face. Unexpectedly, he bent down and hugged me, then he hauled me to my feet.

"You did it," he beamed, pointing at something behind me.

Lying in a puddle on the floor was the snow beast's severed arm. I guess I'd slammed the door harder than I'd expected.

The arm didn't look so frightening now. It was just a mound of snow melting in the warmth of the Eternal Flame. It was as harmless as a snowman.

"Let's go," Daniel said. "We're not out of danger yet." He patted my back gently. "But you did good, Emily.

You're a human battering ram."

I smiled weakly at him. My head still ached, but I felt proud of what I'd done and appreciated his words. *Maybe next time there's trouble*, I thought hopefully, *I won't be sent to my room.*

"Ladies first," he smiled, pointing at the passage behind the bookshelf.

I smirked. "You just don't want a human battering ram behind you," I teased.

He whistled and tried to look innocent.

Just as I was about to enter the passage, I glanced at the snow beast's melting arm again and n idea popped into my head. If the Eternal Flame torch could melt a snow beast's arm, maybe it could melt a whole snow beast.

My eyes shifted to the flickering torch thoughtfully, then I took it from over the fireplace. Daniel watched me curiously but didn't say a word.

I'm glad he didn't. Taking that torch was the best decision of my life.

Daniel's Hideout

13

With the Eternal Flame clutched in my hand, I led the way down the narrow passage behind the bookshelf. I went first because I held the torch, not because I knew the way.

The passage sloped downward and curved sharply to the left. When I was sure we'd walked in a full circle, it ended at a tall, slender door.

"Old storage cellar," Daniel announced. As I reached for the door's handle, he added, "I wouldn't touch that if I were you."

I froze with my hand an inch from the handle.

"Why not, afraid I'll break it?" I joked, assuming he was still teasing me about being a human battering ram.

He chuckled. "Hardly! The door's booby-trapped."

I squinted. "Why would a cellar door be booby-trapped?"

"It's an *old* storage cellar," he repeated with emphasis. "It's my room now. My *private* room. Here, I'll show you."

He slipped past me and fiddled quickly with some loose stones in the wall next to the door. He winked at me when he finished, then rapped on the door in a confusing pattern. The door opened silently without Daniel ever turning the handle.

"So what would've happened if I'd touched it?" I asked.

"A pit would have opened …" Daniel explained slowly, pointing at my feet, "… right about there. A very deep pit." He grinned then casually walked into the cellar.

I glanced at the floor before moving. It sure looked solid. But just to be safe, I jumped as far as I could through the doorway.

The room was neat. Much neater than I had expected Daniel's hideout to be. There was a writing desk, shelves packed with stuff, several crates and trunks of different sizes, folded blankets in one corner, and a strange mannequin standing in a cleared-out space.

"What's that thing?" I asked, pointing at the mannequin. It held a wooden sword and shield in its hands, was fully dressed, and had dark splotches all over its body and clothes.

"Practice dummy," Daniel mumbled while rummaging through a battered trunk.

"What did you call me?" I teased, hands on my hips. I knew he hadn't really called me a *dummy*.

Daniel snorted and tossed a coiled rope to me, then he cocked his head and smirked. "If I manage to remove one of the mannequin's pouches without getting any ink on myself, I know I was successful."

I stared back at him for a minute before what he'd said sank in. The splotches on the mannequin's body were ink …

"*Daniel!*" I gasped in understanding.

He was talking about stealing. That's what he meant by *practice*. He practiced stealing pouches and coins from the mannequin.

Daniel shrugged. "It's all part of being a rogue, Emi," he said, cracking his knuckles. "I have many skills. Besides, I always give the coins back."

I squinted at him suspiciously but suddenly didn't have the energy to argue. It was the middle of the night, and I was exhausted.

Even Leland had stretched out on the floor with his eyes closed. Since we didn't seem to be in any danger, I slumped down with my head propped on his rump.

"What's … what's our plan?" I asked behind a yawn.

Daniel responded but I couldn't make out his words. They were too soft and seemed so far away.

In seconds, I was asleep. Darkness filled my mind and I

did not dream until—

Brrr-roaw!

I bolted upright, sucking in the breath for a shriek. Sweat matted my ponytail against my neck.

I blinked in confusion several times before realizing that I hadn't actually heard the howl of a snow beast. I'd dreamed hearing it.

My sleepy eyes scanned the room and spotted the fire of the Eternal Flame. It burned from one of the mannequin's hands. *Daniel must have put it there after I'd fallen asleep*, I decided.

I lay back down and closed my eyes, but sleep wouldn't come again. The Eternal Flame kept me awake—its brightness and its special magic.

Why doesn't it go out? I wondered. *What else can it do?*

Without realizing what I was going to try, I stood, walked to the mannequin, and pulled an arrow from my quiver. I hardly dared to breathe as I held the arrow's metal tip into the torch's fire.

My hand trembled. If what I was doing worked, it would change everything.

The arrowhead sparked then suddenly flared with a windy *foooom*. Green flames danced along its edges.

Still trembling, I drew the arrow from the fire.

Amazingly, the green flames didn't go out. More amazingly, they didn't burn my arrow or spread either. They flickered on the arrowhead like a smaller version of the torch.

I spun excitedly with the arrow gripped in both hands. "Daniel!" I shouted, forgetting all about being tired. "Get up!"

He rustled quietly atop the pile of blankets. "*Wha …* what?"

"Get up!" I repeated, louder, unable to take my eyes from the flaming green arrow.

I'd discovered a way to defeat the snow beasts. It was time for war!

14

Daniel sat up and whistled a long, low note. "How'd you do that?" he asked, staring at the flaming arrow in my hands.

With a huge smile on my face, I held up the arrow proudly. "The idea just … came …"

Then I stumbled into silence when the fire suddenly puffed a cloud of silvery smoke and my whole arrow crumbled into ash.

My new secret weapon was gone.

"Nice trick," Daniel yawned, rubbing his eyes. "I met a skinny old lady once who threatened to turn me into a frog. Can you do that, too?"

I gave him a serious scowl.

"Oh, never mind," I huffed. I would show him later when it counted. When we were surrounded by snow beasts and his daggers couldn't save us.

"We can't hide down here forever," I said to change the subject.

Daniel blinked. "You're the one who fell asleep," he shot back. "I was packing for our trip." He pointed at the coil of rope he'd tossed to me earlier.

"*Our trip?*" I blurted in surprise. Was he planning on running away when the town needed us?

"We're going to the Sunderwraught Mountains," he answered. "Weren't you listening to what Arick had to say last night?"

"Oh," was all I said before he continued.

"Arick said the snow was coming from Mount Shadowvane. That's where we need to go to stop it. We're probably the only ones left who can do it."

By *the only ones left*, he meant the only ones unfrozen. The people of Willowhill needed us.

I nudged the rope with my toe. "I'm supposed to take this?"

"You bet," he smirked. "You never know. *You* might need it in the mountains." The way he said *you* made it clear that he thought *he* would never need the rope.

"Good plan," I agreed in my sweetest voice, the one I used when I asked my parents for something I shouldn't have. "I might need to pull you out of a river—*again*."

Daniel's mouth snapped shut with a loud clack of his

teeth. He'd wanted to smart off, but his toboggan ride into the harbor was too fresh in his mind.

"Just take it," he muttered.

We didn't speak again for the next several minutes. Daniel shuffled through his boxes and shelves, considering various equipment and tools. He mumbled to himself the whole time, and tossed more items over his shoulder than he kept.

When he was done, the cellar was a mess. It looked the way a boy's hideout should look. Seeing it that way made me smile, but I didn't say a word.

He pressed a bundle into my hands then headed for the door. "Food," he told me. "And don't forget the torch."

I gave the package a quick sniff and immediately wrinkled my nose in disappointment. Dried beef full of salt. Yuck!

One way to keep meat fresh when it isn't to be eaten right away is to salt it heavily and then leave it to dry. The process is called *curing* the meat.

Cured meat wasn't my favorite. It's dry, salty, and sometimes as tough to chew as a leather belt.

After snatching Daniel's rope, my bow, and the Eternal Flame, I made another long jump through the doorway. I wasn't about to test Daniel's booby-trapped floor.

We crept slowly back up the winding passageway and stopped in front of the secret door in the bookshelf. Daniel pressed his ear against it, listened carefully, then nodded.

He hadn't heard anything. The room beyond was empty.

We passed through the door to find the library a wreck. Piles of books cluttered the floor, furniture was overturned and smashed, and the entry door dangled crookedly from a single hinge.

"Don't make any noise," Daniel whispered unnecessarily. "The snow beasts might not have gone far."

Before I could roll my eyes at him, he slipped silently into the common room and returned almost as quickly. "The coast is clear," he advised. "Let's run for it."

I almost made a sassy comment about the *human shadow* suggesting we run for it.

The common room was still crowded with frozen people. I tried not to look at them, but their terrified eyes followed me, begging for help I couldn't provide.

With our heads down, we hurried out of the inn. The sky was grey and thick with low clouds. Icy rain pelted us in stinging drops.

Walking the slippery streets of Willowhill took forever. The only sounds were the crunches of our boots on the snowy ground and the constant pattering of rain. The town was a frozen tomb.

When we rounded the last turn leading toward the harbor, a terrified shriek echoed through the streets.

"*Arghhhh*—help me!" it wailed.

Daniel and I threw our backs against the nearest building.

The shriek came again, this time without words. It was a pitiful cry of terror. Someone was in trouble.

Brrr-roaw! A snow beast howled in response to the haunting wail.

"Defend!" I shouted to Leland as I tore my bow from my shoulder. The big dog dashed back the way we'd come.

Stumbling and sliding, I rounded the corner in pursuit. When I saw the wall of advancing snow beasts, I fell onto my knees, skidding painfully across the jagged ice.

There must have been two dozen of the icy monsters. They were chasing a chubby man down the street—Mr. Crumbpaunch the baker. He wailed in fear and his eyes were wild with terror.

"Help me!" he pleaded as a snow beast's icy hand grasped him around the throat.

15

Mr. Crumbpaunch's desperate cry died as quickly as if he'd hit the ground after a long fall. His body went incredibly still and his skin turned icy blue.

Brrrraw!

The snow beast that had him by the throat bellowed in triumph. A faint blue glow surrounded its icy claw.

Mr. Crumbpaunch was frozen in a thin sheet of ice from head to toe.

"Get up!" Daniel roared, clawing at my arm. Leland crouched next to me, the fur standing up along his back.

Numbly, I thought of the Eternal Flame in my hand. Would it work as a weapon? Could I use it to destroy the snow beasts?

Daniel noticed my hesitation. "It's not time to be a hero!" he shouted. "Let's get out of here."

65

He was right, of course. Facing twenty snow beasts wasn't the right time to experiment with the torch. Escaping was a better plan.

So we ran all the way to the hill that led down to the harbor.

"This way!" Daniel called, pointing down the hill. "We're taking a boat." Behind him, the snow beasts lumbered closer. They didn't have any trouble crossing the icy streets.

In frustration, I slipped again, landing face first in the snow. *Why hadn't I thought of a boat?* I angrily asked myself. The Longrapid River was running backward. Its current would pull us upriver. We would barely have to paddle.

I started to climb to my feet when a dark shadow whipped by my head. A whistling breeze and an icy wetness splattered against my cheek.

Throosh-tun-tun!

An enormous, icy boulder crashed inches to my right. It was packed so solidly that the impact didn't break it. But if it had struck me, I'd have broken!

From less than thirty feet away the snow beasts scooped up mounds of snow. Their hands glowed blue again as they packed and shaped new snow boulders.

"The toboggan!" I cried, standing and spinning about desperately. The big sled could carry us to the bottom of the hill in a hurry. Daniel had proven that.

Throosh-tun-tun! A second boulder crashed where Daniel had been standing a moment before.

Rolling to his feet, he shouted, "It's in the harbor. We've got to find something …" He trailed off, his eyes spying a way to escape.

A pair of frozen soldiers holding swords and large, rectangular shields stood on the edge of the hill. Seeing them, I knew exactly what Daniel was thinking, but he reached the soldiers before I did.

Boulders thumped all around us, and the snow beasts kept advancing.

Without slowing, Daniel leaped feet first into the air, yelling an apology to the frozen soldiers. "Sorry!" he shouted as his boots smacked into a shield and knocked it to the ground with a loud *kronngg!* The shield landed face-down in the snow with its curved top edge teetering over the hill.

"Perfect!" I cheered, scampering for the shield. "Come, Leland!"

Throosh-tun-tun! Boulders rained down from every-where.

Brrr-roaw! The snow beasts howled.

I dove for the sled and snagged Leland's collar in one motion. We huddled on the front of the shield, my face buried in the dog's fur.

Seconds passed that seemed like minutes. *Where's Daniel now?* I wondered, suddenly feeling like a sitting duck on the shield with boulders whizzing all around. *Isn't he coming?*

I brought my head up to see Daniel surrounded by three snow beasts. Like bullies cornering a younger kid, they slowly tightened their trap, creeping ever closer.

Daniel fought bravely with a dagger in each hand. He spun rapidly, swiped with his weapons, and nimbly dodged the beasts' blows as if he had eyes in the back of his head.

He was amazing.

But it was a losing battle. His daggers had no effect, and the snow beasts were closing the gap. Then he slipped and stumbled to his knees.

"Daniel!" I shrieked in horror. The snow beasts howled in victory and raised their muscled arms. Daniel had only seconds before he was squished.

Tumbling head over feet, he rolled right under the claws of the nearest snow beast. A second roll sent him zooming between the monster's legs.

He was free!

Never stopping, he rolled to his feet and raced toward Leland and me on the shield. From over his shoulder, he taunted the monsters as he ran.

Blocks of ice with brains of snow
Can't catch me—watch Daniel go!

He was showing off, but I saw the fear in his eyes. He was terrified. He had almost been turned to a block of ice.

"Push, push!" he cried, waving his arms.

I swatted the ground with my free hand and clutched the torch in the other.

Scri-i-i-itch!

The shield slid forward when Daniel kicked its back end with his boot. Then he landed behind me with a thump as the shield tottered over the edge of the hill and started to race downward.

"*Woooh!*" he shouted excitedly as the shield picked up speed.

I glanced over my shoulder to see him crouching low, but standing, on the back of the shield. He had his arms spread wide for balance.

The look in his eyes wasn't fear this time. He was having the time of his life.

I wasn't so thrilled. We might have escaped the snow beasts, but the harbor was coming up quick.

And we had no way of stopping.

16

Wind blasted my face and made my eyes water as Daniel, Leland, and I sped down the hill on our shield-sled. The harbor zoomed closer, and snow beasts howled angrily behind us.

We'd never be able to stop before plunging into the freezing water.

"Jump!" I shouted at the top of my lungs.

Tugging Leland's collar, I rolled left into the snow. Daniel dove right. The shield skidded and bounced into the harbor with an icy splash.

"*Ungh!*" I grunted, tumbling wildly—once, twice, and then three times before skidding to a halt on the shoreline.

Dazed, I sputtered and shook clumps of snow from my hair. My body ached here and there, but nothing seemed to be broken.

"Now that was a rogue's escape!" Daniel exclaimed. He was already on his feet, brushing the snow from his clothes.

"Umm, the escape isn't over yet," I shot back, glancing over my shoulder. The pack of beasts was making its way down the hill. "Where's that boat you were talking about?"

"This way." Daniel pointed, and I pulled myself up and started after him. Leland barked once as he took up a watchful place at my side.

The boat was more like a bathtub than a real boat. It was short and blocky with a snub nose as if it had been in a few too many collisions.

Rickety described it perfectly. The boat hadn't been built with daring escapes in mind. It looked full of leaks.

"Did the tidal hydra get a hold of it?" I teased half-heartedly. I genuinely thought the boat was damaged.

Daniel shot me a nasty look. "Just get in," he ordered. "The *Dreadknot* will take us where we need to go."

Dreadknot? I wondered. *Daniel had named the boat? That must mean …*

"You built this tub—er, boat?" I asked.

He glared at me so hard that I decided to drop the subject. Calling for Leland, I climbed aboard.

Daniel gave the boat a big push then hopped in behind me. Water exploded in chilling columns on both sides of the boat as he took his seat.

Spluh-gunk!

The snow beasts were throwing boulders again. They roared in rage from the shore.

"Look!" I beamed, pointing at the snarling pack. "They're afraid of water."

Snow beasts crowded the harbor's edge. They paced the shoreline, howling, and shook their arms. But not one of them set foot in the water.

"That's nice," Daniel grunted, "but would you mind helping me paddle before one of their boulders sinks us?" In the excitement, I hadn't noticed him take up an oar and start to paddle canoe-style.

Spluh-gunk! Another boulder smacked into the water, this time so close that it sent the *Dreadknot* rocking crazily.

I jammed the handle of the Eternal Flame between two warped boards and snatched the other oar. I'd never paddled a boat before but figured it was really important to learn how right then.

We left the harbor behind and navigated our way north into the Longrapid River. The backward current picked up from there, pulling us steadily along.

Daniel's plan was working. It seemed as if the river would carry us all the way to the Sunderwraught Mountains.

Once we were out of the harbor, we dropped our oars and slumped against the sides of the boat. It was probably just before noon, but we were already exhausted.

With my arms crossed over the side of the boat, I stared into the water below. It swirled and gurgled soothingly. The sound was almost peaceful, and my mind wandered.

What had created the snow beasts? Why was the river running backward?

I had so many questions that I couldn't answer. Arick Dragonsbane knew the answers, but he wasn't here. It was just me, Leland, and Daniel. We had to figure things out for ourselves.

Where are my parents? I wondered dreamily. It was my last thought before falling asleep.

Throump!

Something large and heavy bumped the bottom of the *Dreadknot*, and I stopped daydreaming instantly.

"Tidal hydra!" I gasped in terror.

"Foamwhite Frothing," Daniel corrected. His face was grim as his eyes studied the river. "We're about to find out where the Longrapid gets its name."

I followed his gaze and gasped again when I saw the spectacle ahead.

There were dangerous rapids in the river!

"Hang on," Daniel grimaced.

Foamwhite Frothing

17

Foamwhite Frothing. The name fit.

Frothy white water churned mightily upriver. Clusters of jagged rocks stretched as far as the eye could see. As we approached, a hissing sound that seemed to come from everywhere turned into a deafening roar.

Already smaller rocks and debris trapped in the rapids scraped shrilly along the bottom of the *Dreadknot*.

"We're never going to make it," I said, straining to be heard above the raging current. The boat was in bad enough shape already.

Daniel didn't respond but bore down on his oar, which he was now dragging behind us. He had its narrow end wedged tightly under his armpit. The other end angled deep into the river.

A rudder, I realized. *He's trying to steer us through the rapids.* Daniel never ceased to amaze me.

Leland was lying on the bottom of the boat with his head between his paws, and I joined him. Neither of us wanted to watch our bumpy ride through the rapids.

"Here we go!" Daniel cried, his voice difficult to hear in the rapids' roaring.

Skrrrtch! Thumphf! Cronch!

The *Dreadknot* pinwheeled, blasted by rocks from every angle. Icy water and spray sloshed over its sides.

Helplessly, we spun in circles and were battered like butter in a churn. Daniel screamed and lost his grip on the oar. It tumbled into the river and snapped in half between two sharp rocks.

That'll be us next, I thought with a shudder. *We're going to die here.*

Daniel threw himself down next to me, giving up on his rudder. There was no reason for him to risk being tossed overboard.

Droomp! Krisk! Rocks and logs continued to smack the boat. Leland whimpered and whined, or maybe it was me.

Suddenly a bright light caught my eyes—the Eternal Flame! Just as Daniel had promised, it hadn't gone out, not even with water splashing all around us. But I didn't want to take any chances.

Concentrating hard to maintain my balance, I pushed myself to my knees and slowly stretched out one hand to take hold of the torch. My fingers closed around it and—

THUMPF!

The largest rapid yet slammed the *Dreadknot* hard.

I bounced off the bottom of the boat, went totally air-borne, then landed painfully on the boat's bench seat. The impact knocked the air from my lungs.

My neck whipped forward and my head smacked against the rail. Blackness filled my vision. I was out cold.

Double-talk

18

"*Greetings-hello?*" a faint voice echoed softly in my mind.

I groaned and rolled over, opening my eyes slowly. My hand went immediately to my throbbing forehead. There was a good-sized welt right above my eyes.

Amazingly, I was still in the boat. So were Daniel and Leland who licked my face.

"*Bleh!*" I grumbled but gave the big dog a bear hug anyway. His fur felt extra warm in the cold.

No one else was around. The *Dreadknot* had landed on the left bank, wedged between some rocks. From the amount of snow covering the boat and us, I assumed that we hadn't moved in a while.

The roar of the rapids downriver reached my ears. We'd made it through Foamwhite Frothing.

I sighed, sat up, and gently shook Daniel awake. "Daniel, we're safe. You got us through." He really had been brave in using the oar as a rudder. That deserved some recognition.

He stirred groggily, moaning.

"*Anyone there-around?*" he whispered. At least I'd thought it was him, but it hadn't been his voice.

"What?" I asked. "I'm right here."

Daniel sat up, shaking his head slowly. "*N*-no … I didn't say anything."

I grabbed his collar and hauled him down into the boat with me. I forgot all about my headache. "Someone's out there," I hissed.

His eyes widened in alarm. "You mean that wasn't you?"

I swallowed hard. "No," I answered. Daniel had heard the voice, too. I wasn't imagining things.

Now all we needed to do was find out who had spoken.

"Scout," I told Leland, and he jumped out of the boat and dashed up the riverbank.

Crouching low, Daniel and I peeked over the edge of the boat. We watched Leland run into a small copse of fir trees and disappear.

We waited breathlessly for several minutes before Leland barked. When he did, I concentrated on the sound, trying to identify it. His barks always meant something.

Finally, I nodded to Daniel. "Not danger," I assured him.

"But something … unusual."

Leland had many different kinds of barks. After spending so much time with him, I'd learned to understand what most of them meant.

But it would still be easier if he could talk.

"Let's go see what Leland's found," I said, getting to my feet. Together, Daniel and I climbed the icy riverbank, passed through the copse, and nearly fainted on the other side.

A wide, flat plain opened up beyond the trees. It was covered with snow and stretched unbroken to the horizon.

It was also crowded with frozen, armored knights. There must have been two hundred of them—some on horseback, others on foot. They held swords and shields, battleaxes and bows.

All of the knights stood motionless, covered in ice. Many crouched in battle-ready poses as if they'd been frozen in the middle of a war.

"*Over here-this way*," said the faint voice we'd heard twice before.

Daniel and I stared at each other, silently asking the same question. *Was one of the frozen knights talking to us?*

Leland barked once and then again. He was in the middle of a ring of knights, so we couldn't see him clearly.

We sprinted ahead and through the line of knights. A very old man with a long white beard stood frozen in the center of the ring. He wore a long blue robe and a tall, pointed hat covered with stars.

"*I'm glad-pleased to see you*," the frozen man said without moving his lips. "*I am Wizard Ast.*"

I slipped in surprise and stumbled to the snowy ground.

Wizard Ast? Along with Arick Dragonsbane, the wizard was supposed to defeat the snow beasts and turn back the unnatural winter.

But he was frozen. If a wizard couldn't resist the snow beasts' magic, what hope did Daniel and I have?

Old Dog, New Trick

19

Leland growled at Wizard Ast. Not a threatening growl, but the dog was obviously uneasy about something. Like his barking, I could tell by the sound.

I wanted to growl, too.

Daniel and I had thought we could charge out like heroes to save Willowhill. But the snow beasts were more trouble than we'd realized. They'd frozen the mighty Wizard Ast and an army of knights in their tracks.

Daniel, Leland, and I couldn't hope to do better. We were just two kids and a dog. We didn't have the magic of a wizard or the strength of an army.

We were doomed. I knelt in the snow with my head down.

"*Don't give up*," Wizard Ast told me in his strange voice. "*You may succeed-prevail where we have not.*"

I raised my head to look at the ancient wizard. It was odd to hear him speak.

None of the other frozen people could speak. They'd only been able to move their eyes. Something was giving Wizard Ast the power to speak in our minds.

"How?" Daniel asked. "How can we stop the snow beasts if you and this army couldn't?" He looked desperately at the wizard.

Leland growled again and started to creep toward Ast with his ears low. I grabbed his collar. "Heel, Leland. You're being rude!"

The dog ignored me and continued to growl.

"The snow beasts were created by a fearsome object called the Winter Orb," Ast explained in answer to Daniel's question. *"The Orb is also responsible for the early-unnatural winter and the river running-flowing backward."*

The wizard had our full attention now. Even Leland had quieted for the moment.

"Destroy the Orb," Ast continued, *"and its spell-magic will be broken."*

Wizard Ast hadn't moved, of course, but his bright eyes seemed to smile. He was trying to give us a hopeful look.

I stood up and stepped forward. "Where can we find this Winter Orb?" I asked. Daniel nodded in agreement.

The wizard blinked slowly as if thinking hard or afraid to answer. *"High on Mount Shadowvane to the north is a* cave. *It is the source of the Longrapid River. There you will find-locate the Orb.*"

"We're on our way there," said Daniel fiercely. "Just tell us how to destroy the Orb."

The wizard's eyes flickered from Daniel to me and then settled on the shining torch in my hand. *"With that,"* he said. *"The Eternal Flame can melt-destroy the Orb."*

Leland suddenly barked as if he understood what Wizard Ast wanted us to do. It was an excited sound, somewhere between a *woof* and a *yip*. He was trying to tell us something.

I reached down without looking to pat his head. Whatever he wanted could wait. Wizard Ast was still talking.

Unexpectedly, my hand brushed the dog's tail.

"Hmm ... oh," mumbled Ast in alarm.

Leland had sneaked past me! He stood with his big feet dug into the snow, tugging at something hanging from the wizard's belt. It was a bulging round pouch traced with golden runes.

"Down, Leland. Heel!" I exclaimed, feeling terribly embarrassed. The dog never acted up this way, but he'd been behaving strangely since we'd met the wizard.

"Good boy-dog," Wizard Ast fumbled. His whisper sounded flustered and a bit nervous. His eyes were wide.

I sprang toward Leland's collar too late. With a cracking of ice and a shredding of fabric, the pouch split open.

Golden, glowing dust mushroomed in a glittering cloud from the torn pouch.

"*Oh no-my!*" Wizard Ast gasped.

The sparkling dust drifted around Leland's head like the tidal hydra's inky cloud. He sneezed loudly once, and then again.

"Bless you," I said automatically.

Leland shook his head to clear the golden dust away then looked straight up at me. His brown eyes shone with golden light the same color as the dust.

"Thank you," the dog said in a slow, low voice.

My jaw dropped and I fell backward into the snow. Leland could talk!

85

20

"How peculiar-interesting," Wizard Ast mumbled. His eyes stared at Leland. So did Daniel's, and so did mine.

What just happened? Had Leland really talked?

I stared at the big dog as if he were a stranger. I'd always wished he could speak, but actually hearing him do it was more than a little surprising.

To be honest, it was kind of scary.

"L-Leland," I stuttered, timidly reaching out with one hand to brush his neck. Just before I made contact, he fixed his glowing, golden eyes on me, and I brought my hand back in a hurry, afraid.

He was going to speak again.

"Leland walk. Take Leland walk," he woofed eagerly, dashing past me with his tongue lolling out.

Stunned, I watched him leap through the snow, sniffing at

86

this and that. His tail eventually caught his attention and he started to chase it round and round.

A slow smile appeared on my face. Leland was still Leland even if he could talk. There was no reason to be afraid.

Take Leland walk, I repeated silently. *What else had I expected a dog to say?*

Daniel chuckled and I joined him. Wizard Ast blinked rapidly.

"*What an odd-strange reaction*," the wizard murmured. "*I so wish I could study-test it. Blasted Orb.*"

His words cut our laughter short. We still had the Winter Orb to worry about. Standing in a field full of frozen knights wasn't the time to be acting silly.

"Can we use the torch to melt the ice around you?" I asked Wizard Ast.

The wizard closed his eyes. "*I'm afraid not. The fire is too strong-hot. It would melt the ice-snow and poor Ast, too!*"

He opened his eyes and met mine with a penetrating stare. "*You must go-journey to Mount Shadowvane.*" His gaze shifted to Daniel. "*Use the torch to destroy the Orb. That is our only-last hope.*"

Daniel and I nodded seriously. Wizard Ast was asking us to do something more important than we'd ever done. We couldn't fail him. Too many people needed—

Leland suddenly barked in warning. "Danger!" We all looked at him but didn't see anything dangerous. Then we heard it.

Brrr-roaw!

Three snow beasts suddenly rose from the snow like candles melting in reverse. First their heads, then arms and bodies, and finally their legs appeared. They bellowed and sprinted toward us. Their big hands glowed blue.

"*Run-flee!*" Wizard Ast cried in our minds. "*Follow the river!*"

I hated to leave Wizard Ast, but there was nothing we could do for him. Only the Winter Orb's destruction would help him.

So we did what he told us and ran. We raced through the cluster of knights, across the snowy field, and into the copse of fir trees.

The trio of snow beasts lumbered after us, their long arms swinging like gorilla arms. Their big feet thudded heavily on the frozen ground.

"Wait!" I shouted from just inside the protection of the trees. Then I thrust the handle of the Eternal Flame into the snow at my feet and unslung my bow.

It was time to be heroic.

Dropping to one knee, I snatched an arrow and held its tip in the flame of the torch. It flared bright green and started to burn.

I fitted the arrow and glanced up to take aim. The snow beasts were coming fast. I'd never have time for three shots.

Make this one count! I told myself, letting the arrow fly.

Ffft-thew! It was a perfect shot.

Hissing and spitting, the arrow sailed straight into the chest of the lead snow beast, burying itself so deeply that it vanished fletchings and all.

Brrr-roaw! The snow beast came on. The fire and arrow hadn't slowed it at all.

"It was worth a try," Daniel said. "Now let's get out of here." He pulled urgently at my shoulder.

I was too disappointed to move. I'd been so sure that the fiery arrow would destroy the beast. Finding out that I'd been wrong was heartbreaking.

Daniel snarled in frustration and charged past me. Metal flashed in both his hands.

As he raced toward the monsters, something astonishing happened. The lead snow beast stopped dead in its tracks, and a bewildered look came over its face. The two other monsters slammed into its back and fell in a howling heap.

Green light flashed inside the grey-white chest of the lead snow beast. Its cold blue eyes widened in alarm and then it melted rapidly, sloshing noisily to the ground like a spilled bucket.

"Daniel!" I cried in relief and amazement, but he

couldn't stop. He was already through the trees, daggers spinning in his hands.

The remaining snow beasts didn't bother to untangle themselves. They rose straight up from the snow, their boneless bodies shifting like sand blown in the wind.

Daniel didn't stand a chance. He was caught right between them.

Ambush

21

Daniel whirled his daggers blindingly, lashing at the snow beasts to either side of him.

> Look out, snow beasts, I count two.
> Slash to one, then follow through!

I don't know how he could tease monsters and make up rhymes about them while in such danger. He spun and shouted wildly as if he didn't realize the peril.

If Daniel didn't recognize the danger, I did. He needed me to do something fast or the beasts would have him. We'd watched Mr. Crumbpaunch. It had only taken one touch to be frozen.

The question was, what could I do to stop both monsters at once?

Avoiding a ferocious swipe from one of the snow beast's

huge arms, Daniel dove to his left and rolled to his back. He slashed diagonally with both daggers at the closest monster.

His blades connected with the beast's leg, slicing clean through the snowy limb. The leg and the creature fell in opposite directions.

But lying on his back, Daniel was vulnerable. I had to do something in a hurry. So I quit thinking and just reacted. I was an archer, and my friend needed my help.

Hollering without words, I tore two arrows from my quiver and stuck them both into the fire of the Eternal Flame. When they sparked to life, I loaded them side-by-side into my bow.

I hardly aimed. I'd never attempted such an impossible shot, but there wasn't time to practice. This was the real thing, my only chance.

The fallen snow beast stood, its icy leg regrown, and I fired.

The second monster raised its muscled arms for a power-ful blow. Daniel rolled helplessly, unable to get to his feet.

Thwick-struung! went my bow, the worst of sounds. Normally I wouldn't hit a sleeping cow with a shot like that, not that I'd ever shoot a real cow.

The arrows fluttered weakly through the air, trailing green sparks behind them. They curved apart, arcing in opposite directions.

Ffwwit! Ffwwit!

First one, then the other arrow struck a snow beast. One below the knee, the other in the shoulder. Not my best shots, but they'd found targets.

The snow beasts paused to look at me, then roared and charged.

"Run, Daniel!" I shrieked.

Leland flew past me in a blur. "Guard!" he barked fiercely as if I'd ordered it. He leaped into the air at the face of the nearest snow beast.

"*Nooo!*" I wailed.

But his mighty paws and teeth met only air. With a green flash, the fire of the Eternal Flame did its work. Both beasts sagged, slopping into slushy puddles.

"*Do not rest-wait,*" Wizard Ast's voice whispered faintly. "*More beasts come.*"

As if to prove his words, a chilling howl rose from out on the plain.

I scooped up the torch and helped Daniel to his feet. "We need to get back to the boat," I said hurriedly. "We can't fight them all."

He nodded and didn't make a single joke. His face was pale and his breathing fast. The close call had obviously frightened him.

We raced back to the *Dreadknot*, and pushed it from the rocks. The squat little boat was scratched and chipped in a

93

hundred places, but somehow it still floated.

Shivering with cold, we flopped over its rail just as a pack of snow beasts appeared on the riverbank. They howled at us and waved their glowing blue hands.

"Go freeze yourselves!" Daniel shouted at them.

The Longrapid's current pulled us north, and the snow beasts loped alongside. They didn't set foot in the water, but they weren't giving up either.

"We'll never escape!" I complained. The *Dreadknot* wasn't traveling fast, and the beasts matched our pace easily.

"Convince them to leave," Daniel smirked with a nod to the Eternal Flame. "You can hit them while we're moving, right?"

I smiled, liking his thought.

And of course I could hit the snow beasts. They were big and not making any effort to protect themselves.

While Daniel kept the boat facing the right direction, I spent the next few minutes practicing my archery. I sent burning arrows streaking toward the pack on the shore. The snow beasts did their part by melting when hit.

It was almost fun, and we made a game out of it.

"Third one on the left, right elbow," Daniel called.

Ffff-thew! My arrow landed right on target.

"Right foot, beast in the middle," he instructed next, and again I made the shot.

The snow beasts were mindless. Their companions fell melting, and the survivors jogged on, uncaring and unconcerned.

Eventually I got a bad feeling and lowered my bow. "Why aren't they throwing boulders this time?" I asked.

I doubt Daniel heard me. He was having too much fun making faces at the snow beasts.

But Leland had heard. Sitting in the front of the boat with his head low, he growled. "Bad dogs."

Bad dogs? I wondered. *What could that mean?*

My eyes searched ahead for what Leland had already spotted. Two new packs of snow beasts waited ahead, one on each side of the river. Their hands glowed as they packed icy boulders.

That's why the first pack wasn't attacking! I realized with a terrible feeling in my stomach. *They were keeping us occupied so we wouldn't notice the ambush upriver.*

The snow beasts ahead howled and raised their boulders.

Float Some and Fret Some

22

"Paddle!" I cried desperately. There was an ambush ahead. A pack of snow beasts howled on both sides of the river, and we were about to drift right between them.

The river's current was too strong for us to paddle back the way we'd come, and the shore was crowded with monsters. All we could do was build up speed, stay to the center of the river, and hope for the best.

That, and take out a few of the monsters.

My bow hummed and my arrows hissed with green fire. Daniel paddled as hard as he could. Leland growled and paced the front of the boat.

Brrr-roaw! The snow beasts howled. They stomped and hooted on the riverbanks, eager for us to float into range. They had stacks of snowballs piled high at their feet.

Tchish! A snowball landed next to the *Dreadknot*. Water

erupted, spraying me and the Eternal Flame.

The torch sizzled and I glanced at it in concern. For a moment, I thought its flame had shrunk, but I didn't have time to worry about it.

With our heads low, I kept firing and Daniel kept paddling. We were directly between the two packs.

Tchish! splashed another snowball.

Splunk! Glonk! Splush! Snowballs rained down from above like a deadly hailstorm. *Thronk! Clarng!* Several struck the boat.

Screaming in frustration, we threw down our gear and cowered low in the *Dreadknot*. I pulled Leland down next to me.

The snowballs were smaller than the boulders thrown at us in the harbor, but they were having a deadly effect. The *Dreadknot* rocked and creaked under the assault. Boards split apart and bolts popped loose. Water seeped up through the floor.

Throump! A snowball the size of a cantaloupe crashed onto the floorboards, narrowly missing Daniel's head.

"That's it!" he roared. "I'm not lying here like a defense-less lump!"

Before I could stop him, he climbed to his feet and threw off his cloak. Daggers spun in his hands again.

Flailing his arms crazily, he taunted the monsters on the riverbanks.

Snow beasts, slow beasts,
Can't get me.
Missed me, sissies,
I'm hit free!

The snow beasts howled more furiously and heaved faster, but fewer of their snowballs hit the boat.

For some reason, the beasts didn't follow us upriver. Their snowballs splashed harmlessly into the water, farther and farther from the boat. We were leaving the monsters behind!

Daniel abruptly stopped his teasing and looked around, turning agitatedly in a complete circle. He made a disgusted sound and his shoulders slumped.

"I forgot about this place," he mumbled unhappily.

"Forgot what?" I asked, finally taking my eyes from the snow beasts.

We drifted into a wide lake. The shore receded on both sides of us, leaving the snow beasts in the distance.

We're out of range, I realized. *We've floated right past them.*

"We're safe!" I beamed at Daniel.

He shrugged glumly. "If that's what you want to call it." He sat down and muttered darkly to himself.

"What is it?" I pressed. "What's the problem?"

With a wave of his hand, he indicated the bottom of the boat. "We're sinking in Weedabrack Lake. The kelpies are going to get us."

Kelpies?

I wanted to ask Daniel what he meant, but the water seeping into the boat distracted me. The heavy snowballs had taken their toll on the *Dreadknot*. My boots were already soaking wet, and water pooled around my ankles.

I screamed when a dark shape glided alongside the boat and disappeared beneath it.

Tump, came a soft bump under our feet.

The kelpies were coming. Whatever they were, they were coming.

To Bail or Not to Bail

23

I threw out my hands and grabbed the sides of the boat, expecting the kelpie to ram us again.

"Bail!" Daniel shouted as he picked up the oar and started to paddle furiously. "We can't sink here in the lake!"

I still didn't know what a kelpie was, but I trusted Daniel. If he claimed kelpies were dangerous, I believed him. Besides, the shadow that had passed under the boat had looked pretty big. I didn't want to be in the water with something that size.

So I bailed, using my hands. In almost no time they were numb from the cold.

Less than halfway across the lake we gave up. The boat was sinking too quickly. Daniel and I were exhausted and sweating in the wintry air. Icy water lapped all the way up to our calves.

The *Dreadknot* was going under. We couldn't keep it afloat.

"Doggy paddle," Leland woofed, ready to jump over the side. He stared at me anxiously and barked.

With a sigh I glanced at Daniel. He nodded to me then threw down the oar in disgust. We were going to have to swim for it.

The Eternal Flame sputtered from its spot between the boards on the rail. With all the water splashing about, I was amazed that it hadn't gone out. The torch burned as brightly as ever, but I was sure its flame was smaller.

The torch might not burn out by itself, but I was getting the impression that its fire and magic could be used up. I'd shot a lot of flaming arrows at the snow beasts.

I didn't mention this to Daniel. We had enough to worry about just then.

After gathering our stuff, Daniel and I paused to look at each other. Neither of us wanted to get in the icy water with the kelpies, but the longer we waited, the farther we'd have to swim to shore.

Daniel gripped the Eternal Flame in one hand. Having grown up on the Longrapid River, he was a better swimmer than I was. I'd need both hands free to make it to land.

"Let's count three," I said between chattering teeth. The water in the doomed boat was up to our knees.

"*One* …" Daniel started slowly.

"*Two* …" I followed, swallowing hard.

"*Thr—*" we started to say together but never finished.

Water erupted behind Daniel in a freezing funnel. A tall dark shape rose in its center.

I shrieked and Leland snarled.

Before we could do anything else, two scaly arms wrapped around Daniel's chest and hauled him backward over the railing.

"Emily!" he screamed, his eyes huge and terrified.

The attack happened so fast, I didn't have time to scream. But it seemed to take such a long time. Daniel's scream echoed in my ears as I caught lightning-quick glimpses of the creature behind him.

Long hair like seaweed hung wetly about a human face. Webbed fingers locked together over Daniel's chest. Gills on the side of the creature's neck flapped. Bluish-green skin that reminded me of a turtle's belly covered the kelpie's face and arms.

With a second great splash, the kelpie dragged Daniel underwater.

The last I saw of Daniel was his hand clutching the Eternal Flame just above the surface of the lake. His hand descended slowly, and the torch spat and hissed as the water swallowed it.

A large bubble broke the surface, and then Daniel and the

torch were gone.

"Guard," Leland growled fiercely, his way of telling me that he'd protect me at all cost.

Another time, I might have smiled. Instead, I scrambled to the middle of the boat and pulled Leland close.

I wasn't getting in the water. Not until I had to. Not until the *Dreadknot* went under.

When a swarm of dark shapes started to circle the boat like bloodthirsty sharks, I finally screamed.

Last Breath

24

Leland darted around the boat, chasing the kelpies that circled us. Water dripped from his fur, and he barked furiously.

"Bite!" he woofed threateningly. "Bite and shake!"

I almost laughed. He might be able to speak, but his vocabulary was small. Again I asked myself, *What did you expect from a talking dog?*

But his actions inspired me. Even with kelpies surrounding us and the *Dreadknot* sinking, he hadn't given up.

I took off my bow and reached for an arrow. Daniel would expect me to fight. The kelpies had taken him without a struggle. I couldn't allow Leland and myself to be such easy prey.

There was only one arrow left in my quiver. One arrow to defeat at least six kelpies. I'd used the rest of my ammunition against the snow beasts, and I promised to make my last shot count.

But I never got the chance.

Water exploded and kelpies appeared from every direction. Three grabbed Leland, and one wrapped its arms about my waist.

Clawing at the scaly arms and webbed hands that clutched me, I was dragged backward into the water. I remembered to hold my breath just before going under.

Down into the frigid depths we raced. My body went numb almost immediately, and my mind clouded dreamily.

I'm dying, I thought, but strangely without fear. I couldn't feel anything—not my body, not terror.

I was about to drown. Even if I escaped the strong grip of the kelpie, we'd descended too far. My lungs wouldn't hold out for a trip back to the surface.

Still unafraid, I forced my eyes open. The darkness all around was so deep that I thought I might have been swallowed and drowning in the belly of some great fish.

A wall of tangled seaweed slowly materialized like a ghost ship out of the fog. We'd reached the bottom of Weedabrack Lake. The kelpie had brought me all the way down to make sure I couldn't escape.

To my surprise, the seaweed parted like curtains, forming a tunnel in the watery vines and leaves. Bright light filtered through the opening.

We shot through the tunnel and the water warmed dramatically. My body started to feel again. My lungs screamed for air. I wanted to kick my legs and swim but didn't have the strength. I wanted to breathe.

Beyond the tunnel, the dark water cleared and became bright and bubbly. A sandy bottom peppered with sparkling shells opened beneath us. Schools of colorful fish swam through swaying gardens of underwater plants.

A kelpie boy appeared before me swimming calmly. He held a large pink and turquoise shell and waved to me. Then he smiled and brought the shell to his lips.

Seeing him confused me. He didn't look the way I'd imagined a kelpie would look up close. He was almost human, not a monster. His smiling face welcomed me. His wave offered friendship.

Then everything around me started to bubble and fade. The boy seemed fuzzy and distant. Darkness swelled in the corners of my vision.

I was losing consciousness. I was going to die.

My body gave in and I opened my mouth for a big, watery breath.

25

Ahhhhh. Air.

I breathed in deeply, tasting the sweet air, enjoying its refreshing feel on my lips and in my throat. My lungs drank it in like—

Water!

In a panic, I opened my eyes and rolled to my knees. I could breathe!

Errreent-reent-reent. A shrill sound squeaked at me from every direction. When I stopped moving, it stopped.

I rolled over to peer in the opposite direction. Something was wrong with my eyes. Fuzzy-looking fish swam nearby through a blurry bed of plants.

I was still underwater, but that annoying squeak chirped with my every move. A spongy floor and walls gave like thick cushions under my weight.

A spongy floor and walls?

I froze instantly and squinted hard into the water. Something strange was going on. A thin, faintly glistening ball surrounded me. It was perfectly round, a sphere.

It took only a moment to realize that I was inside a big bubble. That's what squeaked and made everything beyond look fuzzy.

The bubble was probably ten feet in diameter. It was also dry and full of wonderful, glorious air!

I wasn't going to die. The bubble had saved me. But how?

Suddenly I remembered the kelpie boy waving and smiling at me. He'd brought his colorful shell to his lips as if he was blowing a horn—

Or a bubble!

The boy had saved me. He had used his shell to form a bubble around me so that I could breathe underwater.

The only question that remained was *why*? Why had the boy saved me? The other kelpies had wanted me to drown, hadn't they? They'd hauled me from the sinking *Dreadknot* into the icy, dark waters.

"Oh!" I exclaimed aloud, realizing the truth.

The kelpies had rescued me from the doomed *Dreadknot*. Without them, I would have drowned in the frigid lake long before reaching shore. They'd rescued me and taken me to safety.

I felt embarrassed and wanted to apologize to someone.

Even though I trusted Daniel, I was starting to think he was wrong about kelpies. They weren't monsters or our enemies. They were just different, and that's not a bad thing.

Two new bubbles exactly like mine appeared next to me, and I waved excitedly. Leland floated in one, barking and wagging his tail. Daniel drifted along in the other.

Unlike Leland, he didn't look happy or excited about the bubble. He sat glumly on its bottom with his head down.

He looked like a prisoner.

Didn't he care that he could breathe? That he was alive? The kelpies were our friends.

Thump, a gentle bump interrupted my thoughts.

I spun around to see the most peculiar fish I'd ever imagined. It was diamond-shaped, a golden brown color mixed with red dots like cinnamon sprinkles on toast, and had wings with holes in them. A long, thin tail flicked back and forth behind it.

The strange fish seemed to fly through the water more than swim. With its stubby nose, it bumped my bubble again.

Thump, thump. My bubble tumbled forward, guided by the winged fish.

The kelpie boy appeared again along with a group of adults. They swam lazily, glancing at us with smiles on their faces and waving their arms in conversation. None of them carried a weapon that I could see.

No, I decided again, *the kelpies aren't monsters. They're just people who live underwater. The world is big enough for all kinds of people.*

Still pushed along by the winged fish, my bubble entered a watery tunnel that sloped upward. We sped up and then suddenly shot through the surface of the water with a *whoosh*.

Ploink! The bubble popped, and I splashed gently into warm water.

Ploink! Ploink! Daniel and Leland splashed up next to me.

We were in a pool inside a sandy cavern lit by moist, glowing fungus on the walls. The cavern was round and had several passages leading to places I couldn't see. The sound of falling water echoed throughout, and a beautiful variety of sea-flowers decorated the walls.

Two tall kelpie adults stood before us, a man and a woman. By the looks of them, they were important people.

The man had a long green beard decorated with bits of shells. He leaned on a polished trident made of coral. It was a weapon, but the man held it as if it were a walking stick.

The woman was almost as tall as the man. She wore a flowing, light green gown that sparkled like the setting sun

111

reflected on water. A flowered tiara crowned her head.

"*Gurgle*-greetings, strangers," the man said in a deep, watery voice. "I am Lord Typhon, and this is Lady Coraleen." He tipped his trident to indicate the woman next to him.

"Welcome to Shoals-*gurgle*-garden, home of the river nymphs," she added with a smile and slight nod.

I shot a glance at Daniel. *River nymphs?* I mouthed silently.

Daniel shrugged and looked away. There was something he wasn't telling me.

Shoalsgarden

26

"Food!" Leland woofed at the nymph lord and lady. "Leland hungry. Feed Leland."

I almost giggled. Leland wasn't much on manners.

The nymphs blinked in surprise. "By all means," Lady Coraleen said sweetly. Her voice tinkled like the pattering of a gentle rain. "All three of you must be hun-*gurgle*-gry. Come with me, please."

She waved at us to follow, and we eagerly stepped out of the pool. Instantly we were dry—our clothes, our hair, even Leland's fur.

Lady Coraleen smiled knowingly at our amazement. "Shoals-*gurgle*-garden is a wondrous place to live."

She wasn't boasting. The cavern was surprisingly roomy and bright. The flowers on the walls filled the place with a soothing, clean scent that reminded me of soap and honey.

It relaxed my tired muscles, and I felt light enough to walk on water.

Soon we arrived at a peculiar round door. It shimmered wetly like a waterfall that had stopped moving. Not frozen and icy, just … *stopped.*

The lady lightly touched the strange door. Her fingers and then her hand passed through it easily, sending tiny ripples rolling across its glassy surface.

"Water," she explained, "so that we never for-*gurgle*-get our true home while we spend time on dry land."

She stepped gracefully though the water-door and disappeared. Daniel, who'd been sulking silently since we arrived in Shoalsgarden, followed the lady nymph without a word or even a glance at me.

What's going on with him? I wondered, worried and a little irritated at the same time.

"Hungry," Leland barked, then he bounded through the door. I wasn't sure if he'd meant himself or Daniel.

Expecting to get wet again, I followed Leland, but the sensation from the door was like nothing I'd ever felt before. For a brief second, I felt as if I was a part of everything around me at once. I felt the watery door, the solid caves of Shoalsgarden, Weedabrack Lake's cold waters, and even the snow on the ground above.

The feeling passed almost as soon as it came. I stepped through the door and was dry. I was me again, just Emily.

The room beyond was round. A rocky fountain bubbled in its center, and several other rock formations served as tables and stools. The tables were piled high with shells of every shape, size, and color.

The room had the same peaceful aura as elsewhere in Shoalsgarden, only stronger. Being there gave me a warm, sleepy feeling.

Lady Coraleen raised the top of a big ivory clam shell. Inside it was something that looked like noodles, but I couldn't be sure because they were a fiery orange color.

"Please make yourselves comfortable," she told us. "Eat, rest, relax. En-*gurgle*-joy yourselves. You have been through much."

She strode elegantly back toward the door, seeming to glide rather than walk. "Once you are rested, we will speak a-*gurgle*-gain." Then she vanished back through the water-door.

Food! my mind shouted, sounding a lot like Leland. I was *that* hungry.

Even orange noodles tasted good. I ate two helpings along with some leafy yellow stalks, seedless white-striped fruit shaped like potatoes, and a blue patty that I think was supposed to be meat.

"Tastes like chicken," Daniel grunted with a mouthful of food. It was the only thing he said during our meal.

I rolled my eyes at him. That chicken joke had to be the

oldest one in the book.

After eating, I curled up on a rocky sofa and did my best to think about nothing. *We deserve some rest*, I decided. We'd been through a lot already, with a lot more to come.

Leland lay down on the floor next to the sofa, and Daniel found a spot of his own across the room. He wrapped himself in his long cloak and rolled onto his side with his back to me.

He obviously didn't want to talk, so I stared silently at him until I fell asleep.

When I woke, the only sound was the soothing gurgle of the fountain. Hearing it reminded me of the water-door, and my sleepy eyes wandered to it.

The door looked different now. More like a block of thick ice than a waterfall. I couldn't imagine walking through something that looked so solid.

I blinked then squinted. *What happened?*

I stood and walked across the room. My fingers brushed the door, and I pulled them back quickly in alarm, letting out a surprised squeak.

The door was frozen solid and we were trapped!

The Truth About Nymphs

27

"*W*-what's wrong?" Daniel mumbled groggily. My exclamation had awakened him. I hadn't meant to be so loud, but finding the water-door frozen had surprised me.

And made me mad.

I rounded angrily on Daniel. "What's wrong with *you*?" I asked accusingly. "You've hardly said two words since we got here."

I was actually upset with the door, not Daniel, but I couldn't holler at a block of ice. Not if I expected a reaction.

Daniel turned away and stared at the wall. He pretended to be very interested in a shallow groove in the corner, tracing it with one finger.

I waited with my hands on my hips.

Finally, he turned back to me. "I was wrong, all right?"

he admitted. "I was wrong about the nymphs … wrong for calling them kelpies."

When he stopped talking, I shrugged. "Maybe the two names mean the same thing? Like how *gigantic* and *huge* mean pretty much the same."

Daniel shook his head and looked at the floor. "No Emi, there's a difference. A *big* difference."

His eyes came up to mine, and I could see shame in them. He wasn't crying but looked to be thinking faraway thoughts.

"Kelpie is a bad name," he continued. "A *mean* name. It's what the fishermen call the nymphs who cut their nets in Weedabrack Lake"

He lowered his head again. "I should've known better than to use it. Me, Daniel the Unwanted, No-Good Orphan of Willowhill."

I gasped. "Daniel, you aren't unwanted!" I protested. "Look at all the good you're trying to—"

"Of course I'm not," he seemed to agree, "but you're missing the point. I know what it's like for people who don't know me to think bad of me. They call me orphan like it's my fault. Like it's a bad thing to be."

I knew exactly what he was trying to say. He had judged the nymphs before ever getting to know them. He'd decided that they were *kelpies* the same way some cruel people thought of him as nothing more than a worthless orphan.

"I'm sorry, Daniel," I said lamely. I'd wanted to offer some good advice, but that's all that came out.

He shrugged and started to respond when a soft *slusshaa* sound splashed behind me.

I spun around to see the boy with the pink and turquoise shell. The one who'd saved me with the bubble. He stood in front of the water-door, which wasn't frozen anymore.

"Hi, my name is Rief!" he beamed. "*Gurgle*-get enough food and rest?"

"Why were we imprisoned?" I demanded without answering his question, frustrated over the door again.

Rief blinked in surprise. "Imprisoned?" he asked, sounding confused. "You are *gurgle*-guests in Shoals-*gurgle*-garden. I am here to take you to the Flowering Friendship."

"What's that?" Daniel asked suspiciously. I hadn't heard him move up next to me.

Rief smiled and the tiny gills on his neck puffed out. I couldn't be sure how old he was, but he looked around ten in human years.

"It's a test of friendship," he explained with his usual smile. "Lord Typhon and Lady Coraleen know about your mission. If you pass the test, they will help you to *gurgle*-get upriver fast."

Strangely, Rief didn't mention what would happened if we failed the test of the Flowering Friendship.

28

Rief led us through the twisting caverns of Shoalsgarden. He talked almost non-stop, pointing out pools and naming the fish and aquatic creatures that lived in them.

"Sabersnouts and wallowsludge-chomps here," he indicated with a smile. "Muck snappers, zipfins, and yellow-bellied puckerups there."

He seemed pleased with his job, so I didn't bother to tell him we'd never remember all the names. I liked Rief and his enthusiastic smile.

The tour ended when we passed through a wide water-door and into a huge cavern. The cavern was the tallest we'd seen in all of Shoalsgarden.

Shaped like the inside of a long tube standing on one end, the towering cavern stretched above us and had a wide pool in its floor. There was only a narrow path of dry land along the walls.

"I hope to see you a-*gurgle*-gain," Rief said with a smile. He gave a slight bow then dove into the pool with hardly a splash.

The pool was deep, clear, and full of fish. Thick beds of red and yellow sea-flowers swayed in its depths, hiding exactly how deep it was.

"Welcome, *gurgle*-guests, to the Flowering Friendship," a watery nymph voice echoed from far above. It was Lord Typhon.

He appeared on a ledge along the cavern's wall near the ceiling. Next to him stood Lady Coraleen.

More nymphs crowded other ledges. They encircled the whole upper rim of the tube-like cavern.

I felt small and insignificant looking up at that long tube, like an ant peering through its hole at the sky. The nymphs were almost as small as the dark shapes of high-flying birds.

"I don't like ..." I started to whisper but quickly swallowed my words as they echoed louder and louder in the cavern. Surely the nymphs had heard!

I flattened myself against the damp wall, expecting something bad to happen.

Lady Coraleen spoke next, her soft voice tumbling down like a waterfall. "Let it be-*gurgle*-gin," she declared, then she sang in a soft voice.

From sea to stone, river to rain,
All life is linked; cherish the chain.
This bond that binds, water in waves—
One heart, one hope—survives and saves.

Her song was describing a connection of some kind, I realized. She and the nymphs believed that water was more than their home. They believed it connected all things to one another.

But why explain that to us now? I wondered. *And why not come right out and say it?*

Daniel threw out an arm protectively in front of me. "What are we supposed to do?" he demanded bravely. He might not have thought of the nymphs as kelpies anymore, but he didn't completely trust them either.

"Prove your friendship," Lord Typhon explained. "Deliver a bubblestalk blossom from the pool to our queen."

Guh-bloop!

As if it knew it was being discussed, the pool suddenly bubbled and started to overflow. Water rushed over its edge, welling up around our feet.

"Not again!" I complained, remembering the sinking *Dreadknot* and our troubles in Weedabrack Lake. I was tired of getting soaked.

"Hang on, Emi," Daniel said. "I know what to do." The fierce look in his eyes told me that he was taking the challenge of the Flowering Friendship personally. He was acting as if he had something to prove to the nymphs or—

To himself.

I understood Daniel's look. He wanted to be the one to earn the nymphs' friendship for both of us. He wanted to make things right after having called them kelpies.

"Go!" I said encouragingly, and his smile was a thank-you. He took a big breath, winked, then dove into the pool.

Go fast, I silently corrected. The water in the cavern was rising rapidly. Already it lapped at my knees.

Sensing the danger, Leland barked. "Sit?" he woofed, asking in his dog's way if we should stay or run.

I patted his nose. "Outside," I replied in that cutesy voice people use when they talk to animals. I didn't want him to worry. "Go outside, boy."

I must have sounded convincing because the dog trotted through the water-door without a backward glance.

Gasping for breath, Daniel shot up out of the water. In one hand he clutched a beautiful bubblestalk blossom. It was red like a rose but three times the size. Yellow polka-dots that looked like bubbles speckled its petals.

With the water at his waist, Daniel held the flower up for the nymphs to see. "Your blossom, lady," he called with a satisfied look on his face.

His voice drifted into silence, and then there was only the sound of rushing water in the cavern. The nymphs seemed to be ignoring him.

An unpleasant thought occurred to me. "I think we have to give it to her. You know … up there." I pointed to the ledge far overhead where Lady Coraleen waited.

Daniel nodded confidently. "No problem," he smirked. "I'm a human spider."

Without giving me a chance to ask what that meant, he put the rose sideways in his mouth as if it were a pirate's knife and started to climb the cavern wall.

My jaw dropped. *How can …?* I started to ask myself before I noticed something shiny near the toes of his boots.

Blades! Daniel's boots had small, pointy blades sticking out from their tips. In his hands, he gripped banana-sized iron spikes.

Daniel really could do almost anything. What a rogue!

Watching him climb, I was so excited that I hardly noticed the water pass my elbows and then my shoulders. When it splashed against my chin, I sputtered in surprise.

"Hurry!" I shouted. Daniel wasn't even halfway up, and I was already treading water.

Even worse, the water was building up speed. It swirled like a whirlpool, dragging me round and round. My feet couldn't find the bottom.

Suddenly the current pulled me under, and I thrashed wildly, clawing for air. "Daniel!" I shrieked before gulping a mouthful of water.

He was halfway up the wall when the rushing water

sucked me under again. I kicked and flailed desperately but never found my way back to the surface.

Underwater Wisdom

29

Water poured into my mouth and nose. I was really going to die this time. The furious current whipped me around like the wreckage from a sunken ship.

What kind of friendship were the nymphs offering? I wanted to understand. Rief hadn't told us the consequence of failure because failure meant—

Death.

Through the churning, bubbling water a dark shape approached. It swam straight toward me like a hungry predator.

I tried to escape but the current was too strong. I was as helpless as a fish tangled in a net.

The shape came nearer. One shadowy tentacle reached for me …

Daniel's arm clamped around my waist and started

dragging me along. Daniel, not a monster! He was a hero again.

We struggled toward the water-door, dragging each other along. Just before we slipped through, I caught a brief glimpse of the red and yellow bubblestalk blossom tumbling about the pool.

We would survive, but we'd failed the Flowering Friendship. Daniel had been forced to save me before giving the flower to Lady Coraleen.

"We have to escape," I sputtered once we'd made it to dry ground.

Lying on his back, Daniel chuckled but didn't move.

"This isn't funny!" I protested weakly. "We failed the nymphs' test of friendship. They're going to punish us."

He slowly sat, grunting as he pushed himself up. His long bangs dangled in his face, and he flipped them back with a quick toss of his head.

"No, they aren't," he said firmly. "We didn't fail." The look he gave me was every bit as serious as the one he'd had before diving into the pool.

"But …" I argued without much conviction.

Then the meaning of Lady Coraleen's song came back to me. *Water connects all things.*

That meant the blossom was already connected to her. We hadn't needed to climb the wall or deliver the flower in person. The rising water would take care of that. Lady

127

Coraleen could take the flower herself after the water rose high enough.

Now that I understood, I could hardly believe the test was so simple. We'd turned it into a life-and-death struggle. We should have paid more attention to Lady Coraleen's song.

Daniel smiled. "Get it now, Emi?"

I returned his smile with a small nod. "Thanks for saving me anyway. I wouldn't have figured it out in time."

"Sure you would," he shrugged.

I was about to disagree when the gentle sound of waves lapping a beach rolled in behind me.

"Con-*gurgle*-gratulations," Lord Typhon said. "You are no longer *gurgle*-guests here but welcomed friends. Visit whenever you wish."

Daniel and I stood and tried to look serious. This was an important moment.

Lady Coraleen held the blossom close to her face and rolled it slowly between two fingers. "Unfortunately, it is time for you to *gurgle*-go. The snow still falls and its beasts roam freely."

My shoulders slumped. Since arriving in Shoalsgarden, I hadn't thought much about snow beasts or our quest.

"You have a boat?" Daniel asked hopefully.

Lord Typhon shook his head, the shells in his long green beard clicking against one another. "We have no need for them. We are nymphs."

"However …" Lady Coraleen interjected then moved aside to allow Rief to step forward.

"I know a way," the nymph boy beamed, "to *gurgle*-get us upriver fast." He hopped excitedly in a little dance. "You're *gurgle*-going to love it!"

30

"Love" wasn't exactly the word I would have used to describe my feelings for Rief's plan. To be honest, I really didn't understand it.

We followed Rief to an oblong cavern that had a pool in one corner that disappeared into a narrow tunnel. Two great clam shells rested on the edge of the pool. In each of them was a long coil of seaweed.

"*Gurgle*-get on! *Gurgle*-get on!" Rief exclaimed over and over, pointing at the shells. Apparently he thought the shells could float.

"Patience, young Rief," Lady Coraleen chided tenderly. "You're behaving like a *gurgle*-guppy."

Rief frowned, but only for a second. His usual smile returned quickly, and he managed to keep mostly quiet.

"I'm afraid," Lord Typhon informed us seriously, "that

most of your belongings were lost in the lake. We were able to rescue only this."

In his hand he held a burning torch—*the Eternal Flame!* And it was still burning. Talk about magic! The torch was stronger than I'd thought possible.

I took if from the nymph gratefully, and tried not to worry about how low its flame looked. Lord Typhon's words had me worried enough.

We were able to rescue only this.

That meant my bow was lost somewhere in the murky water of Weedabrack Lake. Our only dependable weapon for battling the snow beasts was gone. The torch's small fire hardly seemed to matter anymore.

"Do not despair," Lady Coraleen smiled. "We will not allow you to depart unprotected or unarmed."

Two nymphs carrying large, open shells stepped forward. Inside each shell was a gift—a glorious bow for me and a gleaming dagger for Daniel.

The curved bow was as graceful as a king's most prized musical instrument. It was pale blue and made of coral. Its length twisted like the spiral of a unicorn's horn and ended in tight curls at both ends. A fine strand glistened like wet silk from end to end.

I reached for the bow gingerly, afraid to damage its flawless beauty. I barely noticed Daniel taking his new dagger in the same manner.

"Riverwind and Thornwake," said Lady Coraleen, and we didn't have to wonder which was which. Riverwind was my bow and Thornwake was Daniel's dagger.

Nearly speechless, I curtsied as Daniel bowed. "Thank you," we mumbled together, knowing that our words could never express the gratitude that the gifts deserved.

"Now, Rief," Lord Typhon grinned, "you may resume your *gurgle*-guppy dance." He and Lady Coraleen shared a wink.

With a cheer, Rief dashed to Daniel and me and started tugging on our sleeves. It was time to see if his shells could float.

At the pool's edge, Rief gave us some confusing instructions. "Stand on the shell and hold on tight," he babbled almost too quickly for us to keep up. "If you fall, let *gurgle*-go. If you want to stop, let *gurgle*-go."

He squinted up at us with his smiling, speckled face. "*Gurgle*-got it?"

Daniel and I shrugged. "Sure," I fibbed. It was easier than asking the questions Rief was too excited to answer.

"*Gurgle*-great!" he exclaimed, then turned and dove into the pool.

Leaning close, Daniel whispered into my ear. "He looks like he's planning to tow us."

I started to nod in agreement when Rief and then two large fish broke the surface of the pool. "Each of you throw one end of your ropes to me!" the boy called.

The fish were familiar. I'd seen them during my ride in the bubble below Weedabrack Lake. In a peculiar way, they reminded me of breakfast waffles.

They were shaped like diamonds and seemed to be mostly wings and tails. They were about the size of a horse's saddle, and their wings were full of holes. Not little ridges or dips, but holes. I could see all the way through them.

"Remind you of breakfast?" Daniel kidded, but his face was pale. The joke was his way of easing the nervousness we both felt.

Keeping Leland close, I hesitantly stepped onto a shell and tossed one end of the seaweed rope to Rief. I gripped the other end fiercely in both hands. Next to me, Daniel did the same.

"Hang on," I told Leland quietly.

The dog didn't speak exactly, but his anxious bark sounded a lot like, "*Duh!*"

Rief swam to one winged fish and then the other. Because of the water and distance, I couldn't be sure, but it looked as if the strange creatures clenched our ropes in their teeth.

"This is a bad *ide*—" I started to say but Rief's joyful shout interrupted me.

"Here we *gurgle*-go! Farewell!" Then he cried out

words I couldn't understand in a strange language. The sound of them was anything but human. They were a mix of popping bubbles and trickling water.

The diamond-shaped fish suddenly flapped their wings and started toward the tunnel. The rope in my hands went taut. My arms jerked forward, and my head snapped back.

Scrint-floosh! The shell beneath me slid noisily from the pool's edge and splashed into the water.

"Rief!" I cried, my voice a shriek.

But he didn't hear me, and it was too late.

Vroooosh! The winged fish on the end of my rope soared into the tunnel, dragging me with it.

Water Bugs

31

"Faster!" I heard Daniel shout from somewhere back in the tunnel.

Faster? He was crazy! I was holding on for dear life, barely keeping my balance. Even Leland was lying flat on his stomach and whimpering.

Dark shapes *whooshed* past too close for my liking, and water sprayed everywhere in the tunnel. I was soaked again, and the Eternal Flame sputtered as if it was in danger of going out.

I would have preferred to take my chances swimming through Weedabrack Lake. I would have preferred anything to being hauled at breakneck speed through the dark by a fish with holes in its wings.

Yep, I decided. *Daniel is crazy, and so is Rief for making us do this.* They were both such … boys!

I screamed until faint grey light appeared ahead. As it brightened, I noticed that we were traveling upward at a steady angle.

"We might make it, Leland," I hissed between clenched teeth. I was thinking the light ahead meant that our ride was almost over and that we were approaching the surface.

I prayed I was right. My arms ached with fatigue, and I really wanted to let go of the rope so that I could brush away the water that was tickling my nose.

Unfortunately, I was right and wrong.

We shot out of the tunnel seconds later, banked hard to the left, and splashed down into the Longrapid somewhere north of Weedabrack Lake.

I smiled despite the cold and the depressing sight of snow. It felt good to be above ground again. The only problem was that we didn't stop.

"This way!" Rief shouted from the river. "You're doing *gurgle*-great!" He bobbed ahead of me, waving one arm above his head and pointing upriver.

Astonished, I realized that he meant to lead us all the way to the Sunderwraught Mountains. Our race through the tunnel had only been the beginning of the wild ride.

Daniel snapped his seaweed rope up and down, encouraging the winged fish that pulled his shell to increase its speed. He pulled up next to me and smiled.

"Ever seen breakfast move so fast?" he shouted. He

meant the winged fish and how they looked like big waffles.

I grimaced at him, not quite able to smile. "Nuh-uh," I grunted.

He laughed. "Come on, Emi, this is fun!" Then he crouched and leaned to his right. His shell cut into the river at an angle and water sprayed my legs in an icy blast.

"We're human water bugs!" he exclaimed.

Right then I forgot all about being tired and nervous. Daniel was going to pay for what he'd done. I'd splash him from head to toe!

For the next hour or so, we sped upriver in a watery game of cat and mouse. First Daniel and then I would take the lead, leaning to spray the other as we passed.

We laughed the whole time, and almost forgot about snow beasts, orbs, and the early winter.

Even Rief joined in the fun. Being a nymph, he could dive underwater for long periods and out-swim the winged fish. When we least expected him, he'd shoot up from the river and splash us, shouting, "*Gurgle*-gotcha!"

Surprisingly, the water was warm, and the farther we traveled, the warmer it became. I didn't think about it at first, but as the wall of snow-covered mountains drew nearer, I finally started to worry.

We were farther north than I thought I would ever go in my life. There was snow all around. *Shouldn't the river water be cold?*

When patches of rocky ground appeared on the riverbanks, I knew that my suspicions were justified. Something in the area was melting the snow and warming the river. Even the air was muggy.

A fuming, hissing waterfall came into view ahead. Steam clouded the air around it, creating a bank of shadowy mist. Jagged peaks reared up around the waterfall.

We'd reached the Sunderwraught Mountains and the end of our clamshell ride.

Rief waved us to a stop, then coaxed the winged fish close to shore so that Daniel, Leland, and I could step off onto dry land. *Very dry land.* Not even a dusting of snow clung to the rocky ground anywhere in sight.

"This is as far as the waffle rays can travel," Rief explained, his usual smile missing. His use of the winged fish's name didn't surprise me. Of course they'd be named after waffles!

"At least it's warm here," Daniel offered, trying to cheer the normally happy nymph.

Rief frowned. "Not for a *gurgle*-good reason," he said, pointing at the stormy waterfall. "Steamwrath Rage is a place of death. Not even a nymph can swim its angry waters."

The four of us stared silently at the waterfall. Like a stationary thundercloud, it clung to the side of a tall mountain, raging down from the heights into a frothing mass of steaming water.

We'll have to go around, I thought immediately. There was no other way. We would have to climb up and follow the river above.

That was all we could do. The Winter Orb was still somewhere up on Mount Shadowvane. We couldn't turn back.

"I must wait here," Rief whispered sadly. "I am forbidden to *gurgle*-go any farther, but you will need help on your return voyage."

"Thank you, Rief," I told him quickly. "You're a good friend." I knew he wanted to come with us, but he had to obey his people, too. There was no sense in making him feel bad about it.

Nor was there any reason to tell him that I doubted we'd make it back.

Daniel and I adjusted our gear and took a long look at Steamwrath Rage. Rief had called the waterfall a place of death. We were about to find out if he was right.

Steamwrath Dragon Rage

32

The absence of snow didn't make walking easier. The mountainous ground was a dangerous jumble of loose rocks, deep holes, and jagged ridges. Sharp boulders blocked our path at every turn as if intentionally placed to keep us away.

We stumbled ahead slowly. Even Daniel tripped more often that I expected. Only a human mountain goat could have navigated that trail without tripping.

When scattered, sun-bleached bones appeared here and there, I was horrified but not surprised. Rief had been right. Steamwrath Rage was a graveyard.

No plants grew in the area, and there wasn't any sign of life. Not a single bird flew overhead. Not one squirrel dashed about on the rocky ground.

We were alone in a dead world. So we thought.

The land rose steadily, climbing ever higher into the mountains. The Longrapid bubbled and foamed to our right. We were nearing the falls.

I didn't look up as we approached. I didn't want to see Steamwrath Rage or its mighty mountain peak.

But I should have looked. I might have seen what was coming.

"How far do you think it is to Mount Shadowvane?" Daniel asked while staring cautiously at his feet. "Maybe we'll make it home in time to have the Celebration of Leaves."

I cocked my head at him in amazement. *How could he think of celebrating at a time like—*

Suddenly, the dead world exploded with life.

Grr-RARRRG!

An awful roar and a terrible blast of wind knocked me off my feet. They hit me full in the face, reeking like the charred remains of a bonfire, or worse.

I crashed down hard with a grunt on the rocks at least ten feet from where I'd been standing. So did Leland and Daniel. Bones clattered noisily where we landed.

"WHAT MANNER OF WORMS DARE SLINK UPON MY REACH?" boomed a terrible, terrifying voice. Waves of putrid heat washed over me with every word.

Gasping for breath, I couldn't answer. Frightened senseless, I couldn't move. I stared motionlessly at the cloudy

141

sky.

"SPEAK!" the voice demanded. "ELSE I FLAY YOUR FLESH AND LEAVE YOUR BONES TO ROT!"

Leland was the first to react. Ears flat and fur on end, he scrambled to his feet next to me and barked threateningly. "Stay!" he woofed.

Even though he was a dog, he'd done the bravest thing I'd ever seen. I couldn't let him face the danger alone.

So I ignored the awful heat and the stench, swallowed hard, and pushed myself up to face our enemy. My knees threatened to buckle when I saw it, and my heart thundered in my chest.

The creature before us was a dragon. An enormous red-and-black-scaled beast from my worst nightmares. Its massive head, neck, and clawed hands stuck out from behind the waterfall. Its tremendous jaws split open wide enough to swallow a horse.

Grr-RARRRG! It bellowed again, quaking the ground beneath my feet. The deafening rumble made me want to run to the farthest hole and hide forever, but my legs wouldn't work.

How can there be so many tales of knights and heroes battling dragons? I wondered, horrified. No human being could possibly match their awesome strength.

Dragons were too terrifying, too captivating, too magnificent. Humans, nymphs, snow beasts—trying to compare

142

any of them to a dragon would be like comparing the most unremarkable pebble to a precious jewel. Just seeing the creature made me want to weep.

Daniel crouched near Leland and me, but the three of us didn't move any closer to the dragon. We were under the creature's spell. We were helpless.

"LAST CHANCE, MORTALS," the dragon rumbled. "IDENTIFY YOURSELVES. STATE YOUR REASON FOR TRESPASSING."

The dragon's bulky, horned head swung toward us on its long neck. "OR DIE," it added with a toothy smirk.

"*D*-Daniel. I'm Daniel from *W*-*W*-Willowhill," Daniel mumbled. I didn't blame him one bit for stuttering. At least he'd been brave enough to speak.

The dragon eyed him closely, its deep red tongue darting out like a snake's. "AND YOU?" it asked suddenly, whipping its head to face me. The heat and stink of its sooty breath almost knocked me over again.

My arm came up reflexively to block the gusting assault. To my surprise, and to the dragon's, I held the Eternal Flame in my hand. I'd become so used to carrying it that I'd forgotten it was there.

"LET ME SEE THAT!" the dragon hissed. Its piercing eyes narrowed. "FROM WHERE DID YOU STEAL IT?"

With incredible speed, the dragon snatched me in a massive claw and lifted me high off the ground.

I opened my mouth to scream but not a sound came out.

Fang, Tail, and Scale

33

"FROM WHERE DID YOU STEAL MY TORCH?" the dragon demanded, holding me close to its face and squinting at me with one fiery eye.

I wanted to speak, tried to speak, but still couldn't make a sound. I wasn't even breathing. All I could do was think the same horrified thought over and over.

Dragon!

"*Arrghh,*" the creature rumbled in annoyance, and I feared it would eat me for not answering its question.

Moving faster than I'd thought possible, it stormed out of its lair, caught Daniel and Leland in its free hand, then spun back toward Steamwrath Rage.

Rocks, sky, water, and scales rushed past in a blur of confusing colors as if I were rolling downhill with my eyes open. The heavy sound of flapping wings pounded in my ears.

We shot through the waterfall and into an enormous cavern. The ceiling angled high into darkness. Ledges and crevices crowded the walls, and a boiling stream cut a path across the rough floor.

Suits of armor and mounds of coins lay in heaps everywhere. Paintings leaned against columns of stone. Books, delicate silverware, and sculptures lay here and there like a child's forgotten toys.

The dragon's treasure hoard would have impressed even the wealthiest of kings had it not been blackened and covered with ash.

With surprising care, the dragon dropped us on a high, narrow ledge. Then it lay on its scorched hoard and stretched its serpent-like neck up to us.

"The torch," it demanded a second time, its voice less booming. "Tell me how you acquired it." Again the dragon's blazing eyes squinted at me, at the three of us, as if reading our thoughts.

"We didn't steal it!" Daniel swore, sliding Thornwake and another dagger from his boot.

His hostile gesture didn't seem to bother the dragon. It chuckled deeply at him but said nothing, waiting.

"Mr. Barleyhop didn't mind our taking—" I tried to add, but the dragon leaped to its feet and roared.

Grr-RARRRG!

"BARLEYHOP!" it bellowed. Then it relaxed and quieted slightly. "I gave the torch to him three hundred years ago!"

Daniel and I glanced at one another. *Three hundred years?* we mouthed in silent disbelief. How could that be possible? Mr. Barleyhop was only a bit older than my father, maybe forty or fifty. It was hard to tell with people *that* old.

The answer came to me immediately. The dragon was talking about a different Mr. Barleyhop. The one Daniel and I knew was the great-great-great-great grandson of the dragon's friend, probably with a lot more greats thrown in.

"The torch is yours?" Daniel asked the dragon.

"Of course it is mine! Where else would Barleyhop have gotten such a wondrous gift if not from me—Agamemnon?"

We stared at the dragon, not knowing what to say next. We'd never heard of the name Agamemnon before.

Agamemnon recognized the bewildered looks on our faces. "You know not my name?"

Slowly, we shook our heads. It probably wasn't a good idea for us to admit that to a dragon, but lying seemed like an even worse idea.

Grr-RARRRG!

Agamemnon roared. "FOOLS, UNGRATEFUL FOOLS! IN THREE HUNDRED SHORT YEARS I AM

FORGOTTEN!"

Agamemnon reared his head and blasted the upper reaches of his cavern with an angry geyser of flame. The terrible heat of it drove us to our knees.

"YOU WILL KNOW, MORTALS!" he continued. "YOU WILL KNOW AND REMEMBER ALWAYS. I AM AGAMEMNON. HEAR ME NOW!"

His great head swung back toward us and his piercing eyes narrowed again. Drawing a deep breath, Agamemnon sang.

Dread knights in deed, black heart, and breed
Swore on their swords to see me bleed.
Simpleton squires irked my flame's ire,
Rousing my wrath, fanning my fire.

The skies are mine.
I rule the air.
Beware, my eyes
See everywhere.

My breath is death.
On winds I soar.
Fang, tail, and scale—
Now hear me roar!

Wizards of war launched spells and lore,
Aiming to maim, settle a score.
Bested, their bones, scattered like stones,
Bleach on my Reach, always alone.

The seas are mine.
I rule the deep.
Behold my might,
Tremble, and weep.

> My breath is death.
> On winds I soar.
> Fang, tail, and scale—
> Now hear me roar!

Sneaking in stealth, whelps after wealth
Dare to my lair, hazarding health.
Foolish, they fail; weeping, they wail,
Never to know talk of their tale.

The earth is mine.
I rule the land.
Be gone, you fools,
Don't tempt my hand.

> My breath is death.
> On winds I soar.
> Fang, tail, and scale—
> Now hear me roar!

When he finished, Agamemnon laughed as the haunting words to his song echoed eerily. It was a dangerous combination of sounds without joy or pleasure.

"I am Agamemnon," he growled, "and I will suffer not the ignorance of trespassing fools."

He smirked, baring his huge white fangs. "Now, what shall I do with you?"

Vroot! Vroot!

34

"Let us go!" I demanded. "That's what you should do. We don't want your treasure, and we aren't trespassers. We wouldn't even be here if you'd left us alone."

I don't know where I found the words or the courage to speak. Maybe I'd just had enough. Maybe I was afraid and tired of feeling that way.

Agamemnon could devour us in an instant. We all knew that. What was the point in threatening it?

To my surprise, the dragon laughed again. Jets of smoke puffed from his nostrils.

"Let you go indeed!" he rumbled. "What else would you have me do—eat you? Bah! You'd be no more filling than the scent of a simmering stew."

Daniel and I exhaled heavily in relief. Leland wagged his bushy tail. "Nice doggy," he yipped.

"Nay, I would hear of your plans for my torch," Agamemnon said. "Then I will decide what to do with you."

"We're taking it to Mount Shadowvane," Daniel explained rapidly while looking at me. He'd decided to keep telling the truth, all of it, and wanted to know if I agreed.

I nodded to him reassuringly. So did Agamemnon.

"Ahh, the Winter Orb," the dragon said. "Surely it is a bane to your kind." He inhaled deeply through his nose before speaking again. "It is autumn, no?"

"No," I answered quickly. "*Er*—yes. I mean, it *should* be, but it isn't."

Agamemnon chuckled again, sending vibrations rippling across the ledge. "You are wise for ones so young. My fire can indeed counter the Orb's magic. You may keep my torch and continue your quest."

I glanced in surprise at the Eternal Flame. Even though Agamemnon had said it was his, it hadn't occurred to me that he'd meant the *fire* was his, too.

The undying flame, I realized, was dragon's breath.

"So ... so we can leave?" Daniel asked carefully.

"Immediately—" Agamemnon started to reply, but suddenly whipped his horned head around to suspiciously eye the mouth of his cavern. "Someone approaches. Go now, mortals. Behind the rock."

Thinking of snow beasts, Daniel and I quickly scanned

152

the ledge. A large boulder too big for us to move leaned against the wall.

"Agamemnon … uh, sir …?" I stumbled awkwardly, not knowing how to address the dragon. I pointed at the massive boulder. "It's too heavy."

The dragon snorted in disgust, venting more smoke from his nostrils. "Such pitiful creatures," he chortled. "It's a wonder you survive at all."

He flicked the boulder aside as effortlessly as I would brush away a piece of lint from my clothing. "Be quick now, and silent. The climb is easy, but the way inhabited by wingstingers."

Wingstingers? I wanted to ask, but Agamemnon had already turned completely around and was charging toward the exit.

A cramped tunnel slithered into the cavern wall where the boulder had been. Daggers in hand, Daniel started in, staying close to share the meager light of the Eternal Flame.

After rounding three sharp bends, I lost all sense of direction. The tunnel twisted through Agamemnon's Reach like a maze. Turning right then left, winding north then south, it snaked its way steadily upward.

I hoped Daniel would tell a joke or sing another silly poem to pass the time, but he was breathing too hard. We all were. The tunnel was narrow, hot, and steep.

The climb might be easy for a dragon, I grumped silently.

Vroot!

A strange cry erupted from nearby, interrupting my thoughts. Without thinking, I grabbed Daniel's cloak and hauled him back against the wall with me.

We didn't make a sound as we listened to the piercing noise echo. It seemed to come from everywhere, but how could that be possible? We hadn't seen anything unusual in the tunnel.

We waited a long time before moving. Nothing that lived so close to a dragon could be friendly.

The tunnel opened into a rounded cavern. Several new passages led up and out, but the ceiling was too high for the Eternal Flame to illuminate.

"Now where?" Daniel muttered, his eyes darting from one passage to the next.

I shrugged helplessly. There were too many passages. Any of them could lead out, or maybe none.

"I wish Agamemnon had taken us outside," I complained.

Leland barked excitedly at that. "Outside?" he woofed. "Go outside!"

Daniel and I watched the dog curiously as he dashed about the cavern with his head down. He sniffed the rocky floor here and there with great interest.

In a few moments, his nose found something it liked because he sat in the mouth of a tunnel and barked again. "Outside!"

"I guess that's the way," Daniel said with a shrug.

We started after Leland. Halfway across the cavern, the shrill cry we'd heard earlier came again.

Vroot!

This time its echo, we realized, wasn't an echo. It was an answering call. Lots of them, like the howls from a pack of wolves.

Vroot! Vroot!

"Run!" I shrieked as something dark dropped from the ceiling. I spun around to catch hold of Daniel's arm.

A second slender shape plunged down from above. For a brief second I thought I saw pale white eyes staring hatefully at me.

Trying to run, Daniel jerked awkwardly as if he wore a rope around his neck and its length had run out. His feet shot out in front of him, and he crashed down in a heap.

"Help!" he wailed. "Something's got me!"

More dark shapes sliced through the air like spears. *Vroot! Vroot!* They screeched, dropping fast.

35

Noises battered my ears like a swarm of bees—
screeches, barking, Daniel's calls for help, my own
screams.

Wingstingers were everywhere. They streaked from the
ceiling. They zipped about on wings of stone.

Vroot! Vroot!

In fact, the creatures looked to be made completely of
rock, like stalactites from the cavern's ceiling come to life.
They were long and cylindrical like cones, and had sharp
beaks at one end and clawed hind legs.

The wingstingers attacked by plummeting from straight
overhead and stabbing their pointy beaks into the floor like
arrows into bales of hay. Then they pulled themselves free
with their legs, flapped their wings, and leaped into the air.

The whole cavern hummed with the deafening buzz of

157

their wings.

"Look out!" Daniel cried.

I didn't ask why. I just dove, rolling hard across the cavern.

Vroot! A wingstinger stabbed deeply into the floor where I'd been standing. Lying on my stomach, I watched it slowly blink its white eyes at me. Then we both leaped into motion.

Daniel was on his knees, tugging frantically at his cloak. A wingstinger had narrowly missed hitting him and had sliced into his long cloak.

He was pinned to the floor!

"Take it off!" I shouted, struggling to stand and maintain my grip on the Eternal Flame. "Forget the cloak!"

Daniel snarled in frustration. The shadowy cloak meant a lot to him, and he didn't want to leave it behind. It was part of his roguish identity.

"Hurry!" I yelled. He could get another cloak, but I'd never find another Daniel if a wingstinger stabbed him.

Still snarling, he tore the cloak from his throat and shrugged it off his shoulders. "We'd better find the Orb soon or I'll be a human snowman!" he bellowed.

I hadn't thought of that. Even though it was hot around Agamemnon's Reach, the rest of the mountains were covered with snow.

I grabbed Daniel's hand and we whirled around just in

time to see a wingstinger knifing toward us.

Vroot!

Down we dropped and up came Daniel's daggers. *Shink-shink!* they clashed against the wingstinger's stoney hide with little effect, scoring only a tiny scratch.

"Thornwake!" Daniel sneered in disappointment. From his tone, I could tell that he had expected his new dagger to possess special magic.

To our delight, it did.

Just as the dagger's name passed his lips, the wingstinger he'd struck trembled violently and spun out of control.

Crick-thoosh! Then it crackled in a wet explosion. Water gushed from its shattered body, spraying bits of rock everywhere.

"Yes!" shouted Daniel triumphantly. I'm pretty sure he'd forgotten all about losing his cloak.

We scrambled to our feet and raced toward Leland and the tunnel he'd selected as our escape route. Wingstingers darted here and there, forcing us to zigzag sharply to avoid their deadly beaks.

Thornwake flashed again and again in Daniel's hand. Water and rock pelted us from one explosion after another.

Leland bolted to his feet as we approached. "Outside, outside!" he barked excitedly.

"Go!" I gasped. "Run!"

Vroot! Vroot! Vroot! The ear-splitting screeches of

wingstingers increased as we neared the exit. The drone of their buzzing wings made me dizzy.

Still zigging and zagging, we raced into the tunnel and never looked back. Leland sprinted in the lead, Daniel to the rear with Thornwake blazing.

We didn't stop running until we were knee-deep in snow.

Gasping and sweating hard, I dropped to my knees. Snow soaked into my pant legs, but I didn't mind. I was too hot from running.

Daniel collapsed next to me. Even without his cloak, he didn't shiver in the cold air.

"We made it, Emi," he panted finally.

At first I thought he meant to the top of Agamemnon's Reach. We were on the mountain's summit, and the Longrapid River churned to our right.

The sun peaked through the clouds overhead, and a long shadow darkened the mountaintop. We huddled directly beneath it.

Slowly my eyes came up, following the shadow to its source. I realized then what Daniel had really meant.

A lone, craggy mountain rose before us like a skeletal finger held up in warning. It blotted out the sky, and the Longrapid River coursed straight into it.

"Mount Shadowvane," I whispered with an icy shiver.

We'd reached the lair of the Winter Orb.

This Is It

36

Gazing up at towering Mount Shadowvane, all I could think was, *This is it.* I wasn't sure how I felt about being there.

The Winter Orb had caused so many problems and led us so far from home. Along the way, we'd met nymphs, snow beasts, a tidal hydra, Agamemnon, and wingstingers.

Was the end of our quest finally in reach? Could two kids and a talking dog really set everything right?

I didn't know, and I didn't want to guess. My answers wouldn't have been hopeful.

"You ready, Emily?" Daniel asked softly. He clutched Thornwake tightly in his hand.

I smiled at him and nodded. There was no point in waiting. We had our gifts from the nymphs. We had the Eternal Flame. There would never be a better time to strike.

Still, I wished the torch's flame didn't look so small and that I had more than one arrow in my quiver.

Daniel set a slow pace through the snow. The longest part of our journey was behind us. There was no need to rush now.

We didn't talk as we trudged along. Not even Leland barked a word. We were all too lost in our own thoughts. And in our fears.

None of us had said it, but the Orb probably wouldn't be the greatest danger we would face at the top of Mount Shadowvane. Like a sword or a bow, the Orb was just an object, a *thing*. It wasn't dangerous without an arm to swing it or an eye to aim it.

Someone or something was using the Orb. And that person would do anything to stop us.

The Longrapid River cut a wide path into the mountain. Frozen snow and ice formed jagged mounds around the entrance, and the temperature dropped chillingly.

"This is it," Daniel said, unknowingly repeating my earlier thought. He shivered without his cloak but didn't complain.

"Any last words?" I asked, forcing a grin.

"Food!" Leland barked. "Walk!"

Daniel and I laughed. *Food* and *walk* weren't Leland's last words. They were just about his *only* words.

I shrugged, moving my eyes from the dog to the mountain's entrance. "Might as well get going."

Mostly on our hands and knees, we climbed the banks of snow and ice next to the river. At the top of the tallest mound, we stopped and our mouths fell open in astonishment.

Mount Shadowvane was completely hollow! It wasn't just a cave. It was like the inside of an upside-down ice cream cone.

An icy hill stood against its far wall, but its icicle-studded walls rose unbroken to the mountain's peak. A nearly blinding storm of huge snowflakes whipped about every-where like bees in a beehive.

"There!" Daniel exclaimed, pointing. "On the hill!"

Hill...hill...ill. His voice echoed throughout the hollow mountain.

I squinted through the snow and spied something straight, squat, and whitish-blue on top of the hill. It was some kind of column made of ice.

The Winter Orb rested on top of it, clutched in icy fingers like the claws of a monster's frozen hand. The Orb was perfectly round, also white-blue, and it pulsated with a cold light.

The ice-clogged water of the Longrapid River sped straight into the Orb like metal to a magnet. Snow erupted from the Orb's top like ashes from a fuming volcano.

That's where the snow is coming from and why the river is running backward! I realized. *The Orb is drinking up the river and turning its water to snow!*

"We have to stop it!" I cried.

Stop it ... top it ... it, an echo followed.

As fast as we dared on the slippery surface, we scrambled across the icy floor. Snow obscured our vision and clumps of ice tripped our feet.

Leland was the first to the hill, but Daniel and I followed close behind. Our boots crunched and echoed loudly.

"Almost there!" I shouted encouragingly.

There ... there ... ere.

Ten more steps. Daniel raised Thornwake as if he meant to strike the Orb.

Five more steps. I thrust the Eternal Flame before me with both hands as if it were a sword.

Two more—

BRR-ROAWSSSH!

Ice and snow exploded behind the Orb, howling more loudly and more fiercely than any snow beast. The surprise and terrible noise flattened us.

In a tangled heap on the hillside, we helplessly watched a terrible creature take shape. Snow piled on snow like sand pouring through an hourglass. Hail plastered the shape, making it solid. Arms sprouted from the mass followed by icy blue eyes and an enormous fanged mouth.

That awful mouth split open and bellowed again.

BRR-ROAWSSSH!

We'd found the controller of the Winter Orb.

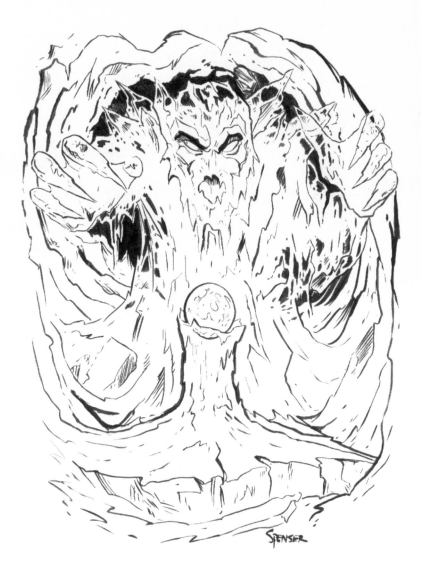

37

The snow monster that controlled the Winter Orb howled and reared up tall. It was shaped like a solid wave and was covered with icicles like the spikes on a vicious suit of armor.

"Yes, insects, bow to your master!" it roared icily. "Bow to Lord Shivasuin!" *Suin … suin … uin*. Every noise echoed inside the mountain.

We weren't exactly bowing. The monster had startled us with its howl and had sent us sliding down the hill. I would never call it *lord* or bow to it.

Daniel had the same thought. "Lord *Shiver-goon*?" he taunted, rolling into a crouch with Thornwake before him.

Shivasuin stared at him and opened its mouth. A blast of chilling wind and hail belched out, driving Daniel farther down the slippery hill. He groaned in the gale.

"Fear me! Worship me!" Shivasuin demanded. "I am Lord of the Ice Morphs, Master of the Winter Orb. Bow to Shivasuin of the Harrowing Hail!" *Hail ... hail ... ail.*

Shivasuin boasted more than Agamemnon, which wasn't easy. *Does everything from the Sunderwraught Mountains think so highly of itself?*

A dagger whizzed over my shoulder to strike the Winter Orb with a metallic *tink*. It bounced harmlessly into the snow. The Orb was undamaged.

Luckily, the dagger hadn't been Thornwake.

Shivasuin howled again, laughing. "Not even worthy of being called a sting, insect. My turn!" *Turn ... turn ... urn.*

Rolling forward like a tidal wave, Shivasuin flowed down the hill. Snow and hail whirled around it in a frenzy.

Without thinking, I dove into the ice morph's path. I waved the Eternal Flame threateningly.

Shivasuin would have to pass through the flames to reach Daniel. And through me.

"What's this?" Shivasuin bellowed at me. "Another puny insect?" *Insect ... sect ... ect.*

"You're trapped!" I said defiantly, still waving the torch.

The ice morph paused and its blazing blue eyes widened. "Trapped? *Trapped?*" it repeated in amusement.

Shivasuin drew in a deep breath, sucking in snow from the air and water from the river. Then it swallowed and started to change.

The icicles sticking out from its body lengthened, becoming thicker and rigid. Its body flattened, transforming into a wall with a row of spikes along its edges.

Shivasuin was turning itself into a cage!

I realized what was happening too late. I tried to roll but was caught.

Shivasuin collapsed over me like a child's hands onto a grasshopper in a field. I was an insect, Shivasuin's insect. I was trapped and waiting for my wings to be pulled off.

The ice morph howled deafeningly straight into my face. Its icy bars surrounded me. Its flattened body pinned me to the side of the hill.

I could barely move.

"Am I trapped now?" it roared. *Now ... now ... ow.*

The echo of its challenge mocked me in my icy prison.

Extinguished

38

Slu-u-unch!

Shivasuin's spiked bars sliced farther into the snow, and its cage-shaped body dropped sharply. It hovered just inches from my face.

I sucked in my breath and tried to scrunch down into the snow, but there was nowhere for me to go. I was stuck in an icy vise and about to be pulverized.

From the corner of my eye, I saw Daniel scampering toward me. His face was pale but not from the cold. He thought he was going to watch me die.

"Get the Orb!" I cried, my voice muffled beneath Shivasuin. I couldn't allow Daniel to forget why we were here. Destroying the Winter Orb was most important.

He hesitated, his eyes flickering between me and the Orb. He wanted to help, I knew, but the smart thing was for him to go after the Orb while Shivasuin was distracted.

With a final glance at me, he started climbing again. He clenched Thornwake between his teeth.

If he can just melt the Orb, I dared to hope when a sickening feeling cramped my stomach.

Daniel couldn't melt the Orb. I still had the Eternal Flame in my hand.

Slu-u-unch! The bars imprisoning me knifed deeper into the ground. Shivasuin's icy body pressed down against my face, bending my nose. Water and ice streamed into my eyes and mouth.

In a panic, I shrieked. I was suffocating! My heels dug into the frozen hillside. My arms jerked upward, trying—

Sksssssstttt!

Still in my hand, the Eternal Flame flared to life when my arm came up. Its green fire sizzled angrily and lanced into Shivasuin.

"*Gargh!*" the ice morph groaned. Through my eyelids I felt its hulking shape slide away the way you can feel the sun on your back when it peeks from behind a cloud. Cool, clean air filled my lungs.

Before I opened my eyes, Leland nudged me with his wet nose. "Guard!" he barked, a command that called for action.

I popped open my eyes and leaped to my feet. I was free and Shivasuin was gone! Daniel was almost to the top of the hill. The Eternal Flame was—

Dead.

I stared at the cold torch in disbelief. Its flame was gone. The torch was useless, nothing more than a charred metal stick.

Instead of saving the land from the Orb's curse, I'd done something impossible. Something horrible. I'd extinguished the Eternal Flame.

Why? I cried in silent frustration. *We're so close!*

In that dreadful instant, I remembered the terrified eyes of the frozen people of Willowhill. I remembered the howls of snow beasts and the dark cloud of the tidal hydra.

Those awful things were just the beginning. More darkness was coming. Shivasuin would bury the land forever.

The lifeless torch slipped from my cold fingers just as an icy shadow rose behind me. I felt it like a handful of snow stuffed down the back of my shirt.

It was Shivasuin.

BRR-ROAWSSSH!

Two For One Sail

39

With a snarl, Leland hurled himself at Shivasuin. He crashed heavily into the ice morph, and the two of them tumbled down the hill. Their howls and growls echoed throughout the hollow mountain.

Leland was brave but no match for Shivasuin. He wouldn't last long without help. None of us would now that the Eternal Flame had been extinguished.

"Emi!" Daniel called from the top of the hill. "The torch!" *Torch ... torch ... orch.* He didn't know it had gone out.

I tore my eyes from Leland and Shivasuin as they rolled across the cavern floor in a tangle of fur and ice. Daniel stood before the ice column, his hands reaching for the Winter Orb. Snow and water fumed all about him.

Seeing him so close to the deadly Orb, a chilling fear

gripped me. *The Winter Orb was cursed!*

"Don't touch—!" I shouted too late.

ZZZT-CRRRIZZT!

Daniel clasped the sides of the Orb and a booming crackle exploded between them. His whole body went instantly still, his face frozen in a grimace. Then he toppled sideways like a chopped tree into the river.

Daniel splashed into the water. His skin was blue and his arms and legs didn't bend. His frozen hands still clutched the Winter Orb.

The Orb's snowstorm stopped immediately, and the Longrapid River roared and hissed. Churning wildly, it whirled at the base of the hill then sped toward the cavern's exit.

The river was flowing in the right direction again!

Daniel bobbed helplessly like a piece of driftwood. To my astonishment, he coughed.

"Help!" he sputtered, choking in the water.

The Winter Orb slipped from his grasp as he desperately flailed his arms. His legs kicked furiously, but he couldn't pull himself to shore.

In seconds, he would be dragged out of the cavern straight toward the waterfall downriver.

Like waking from a bad dream, I forgot about Shivasuin and the Winter Orb. I forgot the Eternal Flame and how I'd lost its magic. I remembered who I was and what I

173

believed.

I was Emily, the best archer from Willowhill. I could save my friend.

Riverwind, my bow from the nymphs, slid easily from my shoulder as if it were eager to be in my hands. I planted it upright in the snow at my feet and went to work on the rope Daniel had given to me in his hideout.

I was too worried to even chuckle about the fact that I was going to use the rope to pull Daniel out of the water. I'd told him that was what I would do, but it wasn't funny while I was doing it.

My cold fingers moved stiffly as I tied the rope to my last arrow. Exhaling heavily, I snatched Riverwind and loaded the arrow.

Like the double-shot I'd used against the snow beasts, this shot would be my first of its kind. I'd never practiced with a rope tied to an arrow. I wasn't even sure the shot would fly.

"Eh-*cough*-Emily!" Daniel choked. He was more than halfway across the cavern, fighting hard to keep his head above water.

There was no time for doubts. I raised Riverwind, took aim at a solid-looking mound of ice across the water downriver, and fired.

Ffft-thew! Riverwind sang, and then again. *Ffft-thew!*

For some reason, the bow sounded as if it had fired two

perfect shots, one right after the other.

My arrow soared straight into the mound of ice, burying itself deeply. As soon as it struck, I dropped Riverwind and took up the other end of the rope.

"Grab hold!" I cried, hoping Daniel had seen my shot and understood the plan. *Hold ... hold ... old.*

The rope hung across the river between me and the icy mound. If Daniel could just reach up high—

BRR-ROAWSSSH!

Howling with rage, a white blur rose next to me. I raised my arms, but Shivasuin's attack was too fast.

"Be gone, insect!" the ice morph bellowed in my face. *Insect ... sect ... ect.*

A frozen arm shaped like a thick club slapped me in the stomach. Chilling needles of pain stabbed into me, and I flew backward down the hill.

The rope, Daniel's hope for rescue, slipped from my grasp.

Insect Sting

40

The air exploded from my lungs as I crashed to the ice on my back. Stars danced before my eyes. If not for the icy pain in my stomach, I might have passed out.

Shivasuin ignored me. It slithered steadily up the hill, a flowing mass without solid shape.

The ice morph was chasing the Orb, but like the snow beasts, it wouldn't cross water. It was taking the long way around the river.

The delay gave me an advantage I desperately needed. First I checked on Daniel. He was pulling himself to shore even though I'd dropped my end of the rope.

Leland crouched to my left, slinking slowly forward on his belly. Surprisingly, he hadn't been frozen, but he was sneezing as if he had a nose full of pepper.

Maybe touching Shivasuin gave Leland a cold, I thought.

With Daniel and Leland safe, I gingerly rolled to my knees and raised Riverwind. I had an exciting suspicion about my new bow.

I'd heard the bow fire two shots when I'd loaded only one arrow. Maybe Riverwind would magically fire even if I didn't load it. Daniel's dagger was magic. Riverwind could be, too.

On the hill, Leland sneezed loudly, but Shivasuin paid no attention. The creature glided down the far side with its back to me.

As I drew Riverwind, doubts and questions bombarded me. I felt silly aiming a bow that wasn't loaded.

What are you doing? I asked myself. *You don't have any arrows.*

With a growl, I fired anyway.

Ffft-thew!

This time I saw the magical shot flash through the air just like an arrow. It raced from my bow, a silvery streak with a faint, watery tail whipping behind it.

"*Gargh!*" Shivasuin groaned as the arrow scored a hit.

Riverwind *was* magic! The nymphs had given me a bow that would never run out of arrows.

The wounded ice morph turned to me and snarled. "Shoo, insect," it hissed, sounding like a wintry wind. "You are an annoyance, nothing more."

Since it enjoyed calling me *insect*, I decided to do my

impersonation of a swarm.

My right arm was a blur as I launched arrow after silvery arrow. Riverwind fired its magical ammunition as fast as I could draw and aim.

The first several shots found their mark but didn't slow Shivasuin. The beast continued down the slope toward the river's edge where Daniel had dropped the Orb.

Keh-bloo! Leland sneezed again. I spotted him sneaking down the hill less than ten paces from Shivasuin.

The ice morph slid to a stop in front of the Orb and sucked in a mighty breath. Its body waved and rolled like liquid sloshing in a witch's cauldron.

Then it melted into snow and rose up right beneath the Orb. The ball was perched on Shivasuin's head like a bird's nest in the crook of a tree branch.

"Sting me now, insect," Shivasuin challenged, its blue eyes glowing fiercely.

I happily obeyed by sending more watery arrows streaking toward it.

To my horror, every shot missed.

Every time I fired, Shivasuin was ready for me. Holes popped open in its body, gaping like hungry mouths. My arrows passed right through them.

Even with the magic of Riverwind, I was powerless against Shivasuin and the Winter Orb. I really was an insect.

41

Shivasuin laughed triumphantly, knowing we were beaten. Daniel was too cold and wet to fight. My arrows couldn't find a target. Leland was sneezing almost non-stop.

Without the Eternal Flame, Shivasuin was unstoppable.

"Now, insects," the ice morph gloated, "feel the icy wrath of Shivasuin!" *Suin ... suin ... uin.*

The snow creature's midsection stretched like a turtle's neck emerging from its shell, raising the Winter Orb up high. Pale blue light shone from deep inside the sphere.

Almost hypnotized, I watched the Orb's light intensify. It reflected on the ice and snow in the hollow mountain, blazing ever brighter.

With a blinding flash, the Orb started to howl like a hungry beast baying at the moon. Shivasuin joined it, and their shrieking and their echoes became deafening.

I wanted to throw my hands over my ears but couldn't risk letting go of Riverwind. If I did, the bow would be caught in the wind and surely lost.

Stinging slivers of ice bit into my skin. Sleet plastered my hair to my face. Wind tore at my clothing and gear.

The combination slammed into me with the force of a solid wall. I couldn't hold myself in place. I was slipping

…

"Emily!" Daniel cried from the other side of the river. He sounded faraway in the snowstorm, and I couldn't see him.

The shrieking wind threw me from my knees and tossed me backward as if I were a dry leaf. My arms and legs windmilled, but the icy floor inside the mountain was too slick. I slid helplessly across the cavern and up the heaping mounds of icy snow at its entrance.

"Daniel! Leland!" I wailed as I hit the slope with a bump and then soared into the air outside.

For a brief time, I was as light as a snowflake. I flailed my limbs, but they touched nothing. I was weightless and flying.

Throoff! I plopped down into deep snow, missing the river by an arrow's length.

Daniel wasn't so lucky.

"*Waaahhh!*" he screamed, flying out of the mountain

behind me. With a *throom-ploosh!* he bounced once on the snowy riverbank then flopped into the water.

"I'm a human waffle ray!" he shouted, clawing his way to shore.

I might have smiled if not for the huge shadow that fell over him as he struggled up the riverbank. When the shadow's clawed hand reached for him, I screamed.

42

"Agamemnon!" I gasped, shocked and more than a little afraid to see the dragon again. I probably shouldn't have screamed, but he was a *dragon* after all.

Agamemnon scooped Daniel up in a mighty claw and plunked him down on the shore next to me. "Surprised to see me, mortals?" he asked with a toothy dragon smile.

I nodded silently and took a step backward, dragging Daniel with me. Agamemnon had let us go once, but we'd had his torch then. We'd been lucky. I wasn't sure he'd be so friendly this time.

The dragon chuckled, a deep rumble in his throat. "You have nothing to fear from me. In fact …" He trailed off and glanced over his shoulder.

Rief appeared, standing as tall as he could on the dragon's back. His usual smile was a welcome sight.

"In fact," the nymph boy repeated excitedly, "we're *gurgle*-going to help!"

I blinked in surprise. *Agamemnon and Rief? Helping us?*

Agamemnon noticed my astonished look right away. "Not we," he growled. "*I* am going to set things right." The way he said *we* told me that Rief was just tagging along. Whatever help the dragon offered would be his alone.

"Give the torch to me," he commanded, and I winced. The torch was somewhere inside Mount Shadowvane.

"It's … inside the mountain," Daniel stumbled, his teeth chattering. Near the warmth of the dragon, he'd dried completely. His teeth chattered from something other than cold.

Vents of smoke steamed from Agamemnon's nose, and I decided not to mention that the torch had gone out. The dragon seemed angry enough.

"You will return it immediately," Agamemnon ordered, shifting his penetrating gaze to me. "I know it has been extinguished. That is why I did not devour your little friend here when he begged me to find you."

Suddenly seeing Rief and Agamemnon together made sense. Rief had probably seen the dragon capture us and had bravely gone to investigate.

"To return the torch," Agamemnon continued, "do as I

say." He hadn't taken his eyes from me. "Draw your bow, girl."

I didn't hesitate. I raised Riverwind and pulled back, aiming directly at Agamemnon's smoking nose.

This time it was the dragon's turn to flinch and blink. "Under all other circumstances," he warned, "you'd be ash for pointing that weapon at me."

Sweat dampened my palms and my knees wobbled, but I managed to hold myself steady. *What had I been thinking aiming right at a dragon?*

Exhaling softly as if he was blowing out a candle, Agamemnon puffed a narrow jet of flame out of one nostril. Fire streamed onto Riverwind with a flash.

I gasped and held the bow at arm's length, but the flame didn't spread or go out. It hissed like drops of water sprinkled onto a sizzling kettle. The magical watery arrow in my bow was now burning with dragon fire.

Riverwind was loaded with a dragon's flaming arrow!

"Now go," Agamemnon said. "Retrieve my torch."

Leland's Last Word

43

With a final glance at Agamemnon and Rief, Daniel and I plodded through the snow toward Mount Shadowvane. We didn't say goodbye or look back. We had too much on our minds.

We remembered what had happened just minutes earlier. When Shivasuin had bothered to defend itself, I hadn't been able to touch it with a single arrow.

We needed a miracle to defeat the ice morph.

Away from Agamemnon, the temperature dropped quickly. Snow whirled inside the hollow mountain, but the wind had decreased.

On the far side of the cavern, Shivasuin and Leland faced off, slowly circling one another. As we watched, Leland sneezed.

Poor dog, I thought, *he's miserable.*

"You're a human dragon, Emi," Daniel whispered encouragingly. "Take the shot."

I shook my head. The distance was too great. I would probably only get one chance to shoot, and it had to count.

Without speaking, I pointed for Daniel to go right while I went left. He seemed to understand. If he could distract Shivasuin, my odds for a clean shot would improve.

Daniel winked at me then took off down the mound. He tore Thornwake from his boot and ran shouting at the top of his lungs.

I knew a morph from Sunderwraught
That ruled the world, or so it thought,
With ice and sleet and hail and snow.
Too bad it missed the dragon blow!

"Dan—" I shouted but bit my tongue before finishing. Daniel was doing exactly what I needed—causing a distraction, a *big* one.

I crept farther into the mountain, heading wide to the left. Daniel was making so much noise that I didn't bother to tiptoe or hide as I went.

Shivasuin turned its attention to Daniel. Raising the Winter Orb, it fired a hissing blue beam from the center of the sphere.

Sssssku! The beam arced like a lightning bolt, blasting into the ice at Daniel's feet.

Daniel rolled in a somersault, just managing to avoid the shot. Snow and ice exploded behind him, but he was back on his feet and running in one motion.

"You'll have to do better than that, Shiver-goon!" he taunted breathlessly.

Shivasuin howled and fired again and again. *Sssssku! Sssssku!* Blue bolts streaked across the cavern. Chunks of ice and rock filled the air. Through it all, I could still hear Leland sneezing.

Hang on, Daniel, I begged silently. I was almost in position.

Finally, I reached the hill where the ice column stood and threw myself down to the ground. I had a clear path to the monster.

Of course, that's right when Daniel's luck ran out.

Leaping high to avoid another bolt, he landed awkwardly on an ankle and twisted it. He grunted in pain as he tumbled to the ground, clutching his leg.

Shivasuin roared victoriously and sent out another blast.

Sssssku! The beam struck Daniel square in the chest. It splashed like spilled water and quickly spread over his whole body, forming an icy prison around him. Daniel was instantly frozen in a cocoon of ice!

I immediately forgot all about sneaking and being quiet. I leaped to my feet and took aim. Shivasuin had to be stopped!

"Surrender!" I shouted, Riverwind drawn to my ear. Dragon fire sparked and spat along its arrow.

Shivasuin never slowed. Turning from Daniel, it slithered toward me with incredible speed. A storm of snow raged in its wake.

Like a swarm of angry bees all trying to sting the same target, snowflakes, sleet, and hail piled onto the monster. As they did, it grew and grew. When it crested the hilltop, Shivasuin was three times its previous size.

"Insect!" it roared, blowing a freezing gale into my face. "I will squish you!" *You ... you ... u.*

Terrified, I lost my footing on the ice and fell. Riverwind slipped from my grasp.

Above me, Shivasuin hefted the Winter Orb to crush me. Icicles erupted from the monster's snarling mouth, and I screamed.

That was when Leland came to my rescue.

From the corner of my eye, I spotted him on the hillside. He crept forward with his ears flat, growling between sneezes. A golden cloud glittered about his head.

Wizard Ast's magic dust! I realized. *But what is it doing?* Leland had inhaled it more than a day before.

The dog sneezed again, and I had my answer. Leland didn't have a cold. He was sneezing out Wizard Ast's magic dust.

Slowly, the cloud around the dog's head drifted apart.

Tiny bits of golden dust sparkled across the hilltop like a swarm of fireflies.

They were the distraction I needed.

Counting on Wizard Ast's magic, I shouted to Leland and dove toward Riverwind.

"Speak, boy! What's your favorite trick?"

As my hands clasped my bow, Leland spoke. "Fetch!" he barked, and voices exploded all over the hilltop.

"*Fetch!*" they repeated. "*Fetch! Fetch!*"

Every single grain of golden dust imitated Leland. One at a time, they repeated his word and then winked into nothingness.

The result was a thousand tiny voices—a thousand *thousand*—speaking from everywhere.

Shivasuin wailed in confusion, spinning in circles and swatting at the motes of dust as if they were flies.

"*Fetch! Fetch!*" the voices barked.

Calmly, I brought up Riverwind, drew back, and fired. The ice morph never saw the flaming shot coming.

Ffft-thew!

Homecoming?

44

"Now we're both human dragons!" Daniel cried excitedly, spreading his arms like wings.

I didn't agree, but I wasn't about to argue. I was concentrating too hard on hanging on for dear life.

We were on Agamemnon's scaled back, soaring hundreds of feet in the air. The Longrapid River twisted along beneath us, and wide plains rolled gently ahead. The river was flowing down the mountain the way it was supposed to. The snow on the ground was already beginning to melt.

We'd done it, turned back winter and rid the land of snow beasts. The threat of the Winter Orb was over, and Shivasuin was gone. One shot of dragon fire had defeated the icy monster.

It should have been easier. Or harder, depending on how you looked at it.

I was just glad that it was over. I'd banged my head and been tossed around so many times in the last couple of days that all I could think of was a hot bath and a long nap. A week-long nap.

Daniel kept chattering about being heroes, but I didn't pay any attention. I didn't have the energy to be a hero. I just wanted to be Emily again.

Just north of Willowhill, Agamemnon landed on a dry patch of ground. Snow clung here and there in the shade of willow trees, but even this was melting. Autumn was returning.

The dragon placed Leland next to us then looked at me. "The honor is yours, girl. Hold out the torch."

From my belt, I unhooked the extinguished Eternal Flame and raised it above my head. Agamemnon puffed a small breath, and the torch started to burn with green fire again.

"Return it to Barleyhop," the dragon commanded, stretching his great wings and preparing to leap into the air.

Before he did, he stared down at us seriously. "Instruct him to take better care of it. My eyes see everywhere."

With a thunderous flap of his powerful wings, he soared into the sky. "I will return the Orb to its rightful owners beyond the mountains. Farewell, mortals," he rumbled.

Daniel and I sighed at the same time. It felt good to be on the ground again. Agamemnon had flown us all the way from Mount Shadowvane with only a brief stop outside

Shoalsgarden.

Rief hadn't wanted to leave us, but his people were anxious to see him again. He'd promised to visit as soon as he could.

We watched the sky for a long time before starting up the hill and into town. Daniel leaned heavily on my shoulder because of his injured ankle. Leland padded alongside quietly. Halfway up, a familiar voice called eagerly to us.

"Greetings-hello!" The voice belonged to Wizard Ast. Walking with a tall staff, he tottered slowly down the hill. Behind him followed Arick Dragonsbane, my parents, Mr. Barleyhop, and a boy I'd never met before.

I don't know enough words to describe how I felt at seeing my parents. They were safe and unfrozen. I'd never been so happy in my life.

Mr. Barleyhop squeezed Daniel in a tight bear hug and patted him solidly on the back.

"I'm a human teddy bear," Daniel gasped just loud enough for me to hear. He was pretending to be embarrassed, but I knew what he was thinking.

Unwanted orphans didn't get that much attention. Daniel had come home to his family as much as I had.

"Well, now," Wizard Ast finally interrupted, "it's a relief-blessing to see you both safe. The land-world needs more heroes like you."

I glanced at him suspiciously. He sounded as if he was

trying to butter us up.

Arick stepped forward next.

"The world needs you now, in fact," the big warrior stated seriously in his deep voice. "Along with this young man, you have been summoned." He pointed a large hand at the boy I didn't know.

The boy smiled and gave a slight nod, then Arick continued. "This is Jasiah Dragonsbane, my nephew. In the coming weeks, you will become fast friends."

Daniel and I glanced at each other curiously. What was Arick talking about? *Summoned? In the coming weeks?*

"A quest," Wizard Ast answered our silent question, "for the pieces-parts of the Dragonsbane Horn."

I stumbled back and saw Daniel cringe. The wizard was talking about sending us off on another adventure before we'd even gotten home from our first.

What about a celebration? What about being named heroes? Everyone from Willowhill must be eager to see us.

What about my week's nap?

"*Arr-oof!*" Leland barked, saying in dog-speak exactly what I'd been thinking.

For the first time ever I was glad he couldn't talk. I knew that bark, and it wasn't very polite.

The End

Knightscares Adventures

#1: Cauldron Cooker's Night
#2: Skull in the Birdcage
#3: Early Winter's Orb

The Dragonsbane Horn Trilogy

#4: Voyage to Silvermight
#5: Trek Through Tangleroot
#6: Hunt for Hollowdeep

#7: The Ninespire Experiment *(Coming Soon)*

Want Free Knightscares ?

Join the Official Knightscares Fan Club Today!

www.knightscares.com

Get the latest news and info on Knightscares from the co-wizards, David and Charlie.

Join the Free Fan Club
Get Your Name on the Knightscares Website
Preview Upcoming Adventures
Invite the Authors to Your School
Meet the Writers
Lots More!

Knightscares #4:
Voyage to Silvermight

Special Preview

1

I saw them when I closed my eyes. Their dark shapes blacker than night. Their fiery yellow eyes blazing like comets. They were coming for me.

Searching …

Hunting …

Their damp, stale breath tickled the back of my neck like a chilly breeze shivering through a graveyard. It smelled of dead leaves, wet soil, and worms.

They would catch me, and I knew their name.

Shaddim.

Shadows of night, groaning ghosts. They were coming for me.

"Just one more hour, lads."

Uncle Arick's deep voice interrupted my gloomy thoughts, and I blinked in the fading light of dusk.

It was getting dark, but I could see just fine. Darkness

didn't blind my eyes. Even in the tiniest bit of starlight, I could see almost as well as I did at noon.

It was night that worried me. Night and what it brought with it. Shaddim prowled when the sun went down, slinking like thieves between shadows. They would catch me if we didn't reach Tiller's Field soon.

"Will your backside hold out, Jasiah?" Uncle Arick asked, turning to grin at me.

Seated ahead of me, Kadze chuckled at my uncle's joke. He and I rode a few yards behind my uncle, sharing a horse and saddle. The seating didn't make for the most comfortable ride, and worrying about shaddim didn't help.

I wasn't a good rider, but our horse Chet was patient and calm. The last thing I needed was someone reminding me of how sore my backside should be from bouncing in a saddle.

"Aye, Mr. Dragonsbane, we're fine," Kadze said to my uncle. *"Even rolling downhill, a round stone will bump and bounce."*

Hearing that, I couldn't keep from groaning. Kadze talked in riddles a lot. He called them *proverbs* and claimed they were very old and full of wisdom.

I scrunched up my face and scowled. *That's what you think*, I silently grumped at the back of his bald head. *The shaddim aren't hunting you.*

That was the problem. To Kadze, we were just traveling

196

along Wagonwheel Road in the evening. He didn't share my troubles. He had his own mission. He didn't *feel* the shaddim coming.

I was on our way to see the famous Wizard Ast. Kids like me had been summoned from all over the kingdom to meet with him. He had news about a very important quest.

The quest had something to do with a magical instrument called the Dragonsbane Horn. When blown, the Horn would hypnotize every dragon that heard the sound. It was old, powerful, and dangerous.

My name is Dragonsbane, too. Jasiah Dragonsbane. But I'm not old, powerful, or dangerous. I'm an eleven year old boy with brown hair and brown eyes. I'm short and I don't look any older than nine.

Except for being able to see in the dark and hear a cat's tail swishing from across a room, I'm a pretty regular kid. Definitely not someone who'd go on a quest like a hero. I can't use a sword, cast spells, or fire a bow.

That's why it didn't make sense for the shaddim to be after me. How could I be a threat to them? What did they want?

Ooowhooo-ooh-ooo.

A ghostly moan slithered in from the darkness, coming from everywhere at once. The creepy noise prickled the hairs on the back of my neck.

Uncle Arick immediately threw up a big hand. "Halt!"

he hissed between clenched teeth. Then the dreadful moan came again.

Kadze pulled up rein and slid silently from the saddle. "No—!" I started but the word died on my lips.

Ooowhooo-ooh-ooo.

A pack of shaddim appeared, floating just above the ground. They materialized from the darkness like ghosts. There were at least twenty of them, and they had us surrounded.

For an instant, I froze with fear. My limbs trembled and my eyes stared, watching in terror as the black creatures glided closer. Then finally, I found my voice.

"Shaddim!" I cried too late.

The shaddim weren't hunting anymore. They'd found me.

2

"Get behind me!" Uncle Arick roared, leaping from his saddle into a battle-ready stance. In his fists, he gripped a wicked-looking harpoon.

The shaddim drifted nearer, steadily tightening their circle around us. The closer they got, the louder and more frenzied their moaning became.

Ooowhooo-ooh-ooo.

The shaddim were ghosts and darker than anything I'd ever seen. They were shaped like tall, narrow triangles, and reminded me of wisps of smoke with curling, snake tails where their legs and feet should be. Their long arms looked stretched-out and ended in scissor blade claws the length of my forearm.

Their shining yellow eyes stared at me. Their mouths gaped, moaning, showing what was behind them like I open windows. The monsters were hollow and razor-thin.

Ooowhooo-ooh-ooo.

Their noise deafened me. It echoed in my mind and whispered greedily. *Give us the Horn*, it seemed to say. *Mother wants the Horn.*

"Jasiah, look out!" Kadze cried suddenly.

A shaddim's dark, thin arm snapped at me like a tentacle. Razor-like claws whisked inches from my face.

Then Kadze was there, leaping between me and the monster. He was fast, very fast. His arms and legs sliced through the air in a blur like a knight's deadly weapons.

I twisted away, pulling hard on Chet's reins. In a stuttering lurch, we nearly bowled Uncle Arick over.

He held a cluster of shaddim at bay with his mighty harpoon, slashing threateningly at the monsters as they tried to advance.

From the corner of his eye, he spotted me. "Don't let them touch you!" he warned without taking his eyes from the shaddim. "One touch will put you to sleep."

Chet fidgeted nervously. He was well-trained and brave, but the constant moaning still scared him. He would run soon, and I wouldn't be able to stop him.

"What do I do?" I wailed helplessly.

A shaddim struck at Uncle Arick before my uncle could respond. His harpoon took the creature at the elbow, passing through the arm as if it were fog.

Unharmed, the monster moaned louder and lashed out

with its arm again.

"Run, Jasiah!" my uncle ordered. "Run to Tiller's Field and find Wizard Ast."

I blinked in shock. I wasn't a hero, but I still knew right from wrong. "I can't! I can't leave—" I tried to protest.

Bending suddenly at the knees, Uncle Arick parried another shaddim attack. Then with one hand, he pulled something bulky from a sack on his belt.

"Take this and go," he commanded. "This quest is about you. Go, now!"

He tossed the object to me, and I clumsily caught it while struggling to maintain my grip on the reins. The object was an oversized, right-handed gauntlet made of heavy leather.

I wanted to ask what I was supposed to do with it but didn't have the time. Uncle Arick swatted Chet on the rump and sent us charging though the ranks of the shaddim.

A tangle of whip-like arms and claws swatted at us. Empty mouths split wide and moaned. I squeezed my eyes shut and held my breath. We were dodging death at breakneck speed.

Ooowhooo-ooh-ooo.

Not until the moaning died did I open my eyes and risk a glance backward.

Uncle Arick stood in the center of the road, completely surrounded. The blade on his enormous harpoon flashed again and again.

Behind him lay Kadze. The boy's chest rose and fell with the breathing of sleep, but other than that, he didn't move.

When I saw my uncle trip and go down, I buried my face in Chet's mane and shrieked without a sound. There was nothing else I could do.

We charged into the night, hunted and alone.

3

What have I done? What have I done? I asked myself
guiltily with every step westward. Cool autumn wind
buffeted my face but my cheeks burned warmly with
shame.

I'd left my uncle and friend in danger. I'd left them to
die.

They had stayed behind to fight while I had run away.
They'd sacrificed themselves so that I could escape. *Why?*

The mysterious answer came to me right away. *This
quest is about you*, Uncle Arick had said. How I wished I
knew what that meant!

I pulled up rein and turned back to peer down
Wagonwheel Road. Uncle Arick and Kadze were somewhere in the deepening gloom, probably fighting for their
lives. Maybe Kadze was still unconscious. Maybe Uncle
Arick was now, too.

I wanted to race back to save them, and I wanted to hide in a place where I could never be found. Not by shaddim. Not by wizards and their quests. But I couldn't make myself move. I was frozen with fear and indecision.

Uncle Arick's words repeated in my head, and I tried desperately to understand them.

How is the quest about me? Because I have the same name as the Horn? If that's true, the quest should be about Uncle Arick. His name was Dragonsbane, too.

Nothing was making much sense, and I shook my head angrily. Confusing images flashed in my mind. Attacking shaddim. Kadze charging to my rescue. Uncle Arick telling me to run and giving me—

The gauntlet! It was still in my hand.

I stared at it thoughtfully for only a moment. There was no way I'd let a second mystery add to my confusion. I slid it onto my hand and strapped it on with barely a thought.

The gauntlet was dark brown and covered with lighter streaks like scratch marks. It was also much too big for me and hung limply from my arm like the baggy clothing on a scarecrow. It reached all the way to my shoulder.

I studied the scratches on its surface, imagining they were cuts from a sword blade. Then I shook my arm in annoyance.

"Another mystery …" I started to mutter when the gauntlet came to life.

Skrrrinch! It suddenly tightened and shrank, fitting to my arm. I cried out and tore at the straps and buckles that fastened it, but they wouldn't budge. My whole right arm was being mummified!

"What's happening?" I gasped aloud. Beneath me, Chet shifted nervously.

Then the gauntlet's transformation was complete. It went still and fit my hand and arm perfectly. It felt snug but not tight, and covered my forearm like a stretched sock.

The gauntlet was magic without a doubt. But knowing that didn't tell my anything helpful. It was more of a mystery now than when I'd put it on.

Thwitch!

The sound of a snapping stick echoed sharply nearby. Muffled voices drifted in from the darkness.

Someone was coming!

At first I hoped the voices belonged to Uncle Arick and Kadze, but their sounds had come from the wrong way. I forgot all about the gauntlet and frantically scanned the shadows for somewhere to hide.

Strangers on an empty road at night would be up to no good.

End of the Preview

Knightscares #4: Voyage to Silvermight

Ask for it at your bookstore or order online at
www.knightscares.com

Early Winter's Orb
Word Scramble

evrir phymn _ _ _ _ _ _   _ _ _ _ _

manmangeo _ _ _ _ _ _ _ _ _

getsirginnw _ _ _ _ _ _ _ _ _ _ _

llowhiwlli _ _ _ _ _ _ _ _ _ _

rechray _ _ _ _ _ _ _

het kretdoand _ _ _   _ _ _ _ _ _ _ _ _

delnal _ _ _ _ _ _

wons stabe _ _ _ _   _ _ _ _ _

aldit rahdy _ _ _ _ _   _ _ _ _ _

ricak _ _ _ _ _

trenlae elfam _ _ _ _ _ _ _   _ _ _ _ _

suvishani _ _ _ _ _ _ _ _ _

felawf ary _ _ _ _ _ _   _ _ _ _

rm yobleparh _ _   _ _ _ _ _ _ _ _ _

Knightscares
Play It By Ear

Match the sound-effects and sayings on the left with the
people and things on the right.

Brrr-roaw!	Riverwind
GRONK-WHOMP!	an icy boulder
Food!	Shivasuin
GRRRAHRG!	Wizard Ast
BRRR-ROAWSSSH!	wingstinger
I'm a human…	tidal hydra
gurgle	snow beast
Ffft-thew! Ffft-thew!	Leland
Greetings-hello!	a popping bubble
Throosh-tun-tun!	Agamemnon
Ploink!	Daniel
Vroot!	nymphs

Early Winter's Orb

Artwork

The hand-painted cover art, official Knightscares logo, maps, and interior illustrations were all created by the talented artist Steven Spenser Ledford.

Steven is a free-lance fine and graphic artist from Charleston, SC with nearly 20 years experience. His work includes public and private wall murals, comic book pencil, ink and color, magazine illustrations and cover art, t-shirt designs, sculptures, portraits, painted furniture and more. Most of his work is produced from the tiny rooms of the house he shares with his very patient wife and their two children—Xena (a psychotic tortoise-shell cat) and Emma (a Jack Russell terrier). He welcomes inquiries at PtByNmbrs@aol.com.

Thank you, Steven!